ROAD

TO

BOUNTIFUL

Other Books and Audio Books by
DONALD S. SMURTHWAITE

The Boxmaker's Son

Surprising Marcus

Letters by a Half-Moon

A Wise, Blue Autumn

Fine Old High Priests

Do You Like Me, Julie Sloan?

The Search for Wallace Whipple

A novel by the author of *The Boxmaker's Son*

Donald S. Smurthwaite

ROAD
TO
BOUNTIFUL

Covenant Communications, Inc.

Cover image © larshallstrom courtesy of 123RF.

Cover design copyright © 2013 by Covenant Communications, Inc.

Published by Covenant Communications, Inc.
American Fork, Utah

Printed in the United States of America
First Printing: May 2013

19 18 17 16 15 14 13   10 9 8 7 6 5 4 3 2 1

ISBN 978-1-60861-234-5

For all who understand that back roads are the best way home.

THANKS TO THE PEOPLE AT COVENANT COMMUNICATIONS FOR
HELPING TO BRING LOYAL AND LEVI TO LIFE.

CHAPTER ONE
MY NAME IS LOYAL

SOMEWHERE ACROSS THE WHEAT FIELDS of eastern North Dakota, my great-nephew is behind the wheel of a big, fast, and new car, speeding toward me. He will arrive late this afternoon, we will pack up the few belongings that I did not give away, sell, or ship to my new place of residence, and we will begin the drive west: the second part of his journey, the first and likely last part of mine, one that will take me to my new home.

My great-nephew's name is Levi, and he probably doesn't have much of a memory about me. I can barely remember him from a family reunion fifteen years ago at a park in a steep, red-walled canyon in the mountains of central Utah. My memory tells me he was the short towheaded boy, wide-eyed, skinny as a cornstalk, who climbed many trees, hiked high on the rocks of the canyon, jumped too close to the evening bonfire, and played hide-and-seek with his cousins well into the night. He didn't say much to me then, nor I to him. Daisy and I were just two people, two faces among many, an old great-uncle and an old great-aunt. Distant relatives, distant family members, I suppose, with no claim upon his life. Daisy, by then, was ill, and when the announcement of the reunion was pushed through the flap of the mailbox in our house, she, with only a few words, expressed her desire to attend.

Neither of us mentioned the words, "To see everyone one last time," but we both knew it, even though the doctor had yet to offer a conclusive diagnosis. My Daisy asked for so little. A trip to see family was not too much. We caught a plane from Bismarck and were picked up at the airport by my daughter Barbara and her husband, Warren, and we wound our way to the faraway canyon where we met many members of our family for the first time and, true to our premonition, saw many of them for the last time. Even now, it seems peculiar to me that we met our family far from our home, in a narrow canyon with high stone walls. It seems odd that we all had to wear name tags, mine reading, "Hello, my name is Loyal."

By trade, I was a pharmacist. I ran the town drugstore for forty years. Daisy and I lived within walking distance of my store in a tall, brown, two-story house with a basement. We knew everyone in our town of two thousand souls, and everyone knew us. I was the pharmacist, the druggist, the man who knew what ailed everyone, illnesses both real and imagined. I would drop a piece of candy into the bag of medicine for a sick child, undercharge someone who I knew was experiencing hard times. Old Doris Simpson huffed when I finally added a dollar to the bill for her colitis medication, though it still cost me more than what I charged her. And the sugar pills I gave to Sloan Jenkins for the last twenty years of his life? He swore they kept him going. "Don't know what you've got in those pills, but they sure straighten me out," he'd cackle. "You're better than any doc I ever had." I never could charge John Fetzberg, one of the three town firemen and the father of six children, any more than I figured he could pay; he always lowered his eyes and mumbled his thanks when I handed him the bag of medicine and watched him as he shunted, slope-shouldered, out of the pharmacy.

On ice-cold mornings, with freshly fallen snow, and with frost and ice crystals hanging in the air like small, twinkling diamonds, I often would awake to the tinny scrape of snow shovels on my sidewalk and driveway, manned by John and his older boys and girls, their very life breath heaving and steamy and frosty blue on those below-zero mornings.

We never talked about it, John and I. Not a word between us. He never said anything about the medicine, and I never mentioned how nice my walks and driveway looked on those frozen mornings. We understood each other, as gentlemen do.

But the times changed. A big store was built in Grand Forks, then another and another. I tried to keep my prices close, but it wasn't always possible. And people could buy clothes and food and tires and tennis shoes and cosmetics at the big store, and my business dwindled. The long drive to the big store in Grand Forks didn't seem to matter. It became part of the experience, part of the adventure. A trip there a month wasn't so much, and if medicine were needed, it became only another reason to make the journey.

Finally, there came a night when I took a piece of light yellow construction paper and carefully printed in blocked letters, "Closed for business.

Thank you for many fine years. Good luck to you all. Sincerely, Loyal." I hung the sign on the front door when I closed the store the following day, and that was that. The pharmacy closed. Not much was made of it. People knew it was coming, thought it was just a sign of the times. They mourned a little and told me they were sorry and would miss me and then drove on to Grand Forks. John Fetzberg said those things to me too, but there were tears in his eyes, and my sidewalk and driveway continued to be shoveled in those early, frigid hours. John, he remains a gentleman.

Truthfully, part of it was the competition, but part of it was that I was tired. Forty years in the same location, the same job, the same cold winters, the same searing summers. And then Daisy grew worse and then she went away. Perhaps it was time for me to go as well, go to somewhere different. Years before, I had played bit parts in our community theater and learned about entrances and exits. I never missed my exit cue and didn't plan to start now.

I add it all up, this life of mine, and maybe the most telling moment of all came at a family reunion in a glade among the spires and aspens of a Utah canyon. Here was my family and my family did not know me. I have spent all those years in North Dakota. I have been happy, but perhaps it is time. I ended up wearing a name tag to tell my own family my name at a reunion. Was there a message for me, for my family, for all of us?

Yes, things were changing in my life, and not just with Daisy and my pharmacy practice and my two daughters grown and moved so far away from the Dakota Plains. I knew things were different and that some things needed to end, or at least would come to an end. I did not like to see the old way end because I am part of it, as it is a part of me.

I am Loyal. That's who I am.

That's probably why I was not surprised when Barbara called and said, "It's time for you to move closer to us, Dad. You're there alone. There aren't many people to look out for you. You are too far away. What if something happened to you? We've found a place for you, a nice place. It's very private. They play games and have sing-alongs at night. The food is good. They told us to come in and have a meal. You'll make new friends. We want you closer to us. We want you to be cared for."

I could imagine her then cradling the phone even closer to her mouth, the lids narrowing over her deep blue eyes. "What's keeping you in North Dakota? Mom is gone, and you only have the old house. We have plenty of money; we can help out. Come and be closer to us, Dad."

Then she mentioned the name of the place, Glad Tidings Assisted Living Home. A biblical ring to it, that name. I had a funny vision of old men dressed like the Wise Men on their way to Bethlehem, walking around a sparkling new retirement facility. Maybe they were just in their bathrobes and slippers. Might I become as they were? I felt uneasy for reasons I could not explain. Yet as soon as she said it, I knew that I would live there someday, within my will or without.

"Come and be closer to us," she said. "Closer to your family." Well, I am Loyal.

I can see it now, as though it were written in the "Comings and Goings" column of our weekly newspaper: "Loyal Wing, a pharmacist here for more than forty years, has taken up residence in Bountiful, Utah, a suburb of Salt Lake City, to be nearer his daughter Mrs. Barbara Bates and her husband, Mr. Warren Bates. We will miss you, Loyal. Good luck and God bless."

I didn't put up much resistance, though I would have been content to spend the remainder of my days in the tall brown house on Chestnut Street and watch the seasons pass slowly. To feel the emotions of an eighty-two-year-old man as time gently passes—the huddled-up comfort of crackling fall mornings and snap-clean air; sweeping, elegant blizzards pounding across the stubby winter plains; the fresh green of spring and the hope it brings that all will begin again; and voluptuous summer, when the wheat fields around town grow from jade to tawny to golden amid the mixed chorus of calling birds and noisy bugs and the deep drumming of distant, throaty thunder.

I am satisfied in the ancient turning of this ancient earth and the ancient joy it brings me.

And so my great-nephew Levi is dashing toward me. What he thinks of me, I do not know; what he thinks of his mission to fetch and deliver his great-uncle Loyal safely to the Salt Lake Valley, I can only guess. He is the agent in my new life, but to him, it is likely just a trip from here to there with an old man he does not know, a few days of time, that's all. How I wish I could look upon the frittering of a few days with such insouciance.

He's out there, somewhere on the prairie, closing in on me with each blink of my eye. He is hurtling toward me, and with him, I go to my future. A child will lead them, I think. He is twenty-something now. How can he know what his mission to my home, across the great sweeping plains, is all about?

He can't. He just can't. He is too young. He does not understand my story. He does not yet understand journeys. To him, this is likely just a long trip.

I will go inside my old brown house and walk around it once more. I will touch the walls and listen for laughter long ago faded. I will say thank you to this house, and I will know that it hears me. Then I will hoist my two suitcases onto the front porch. I will look at the Sold sticker slapped across the For Sale sign in my front yard.

Then I will sit on the highest step leading to the porch and wait for Levi to come and take me away.

Chapter Two
By a Series of Strange Coincidences

The world is flat. At this moment, someone could tell me the world is flat, and I would believe them, no questions asked. Let's see. Long line of corn, followed by another long line of corn, followed by another long line of corn. What's this? A wheat field. Followed by another wheat field, and after that, another wheat field. And stretching on toward the horizon, crops and more crops, on a landscape as flat as a cookie sheet. And about as appealing.

Let's see. One more time. Just why am I gunning down a two-lane highway somewhere in North Dakota, on my way to pick up Great-Uncle Loyal, my dear, sweet, kind uncle Loyal, and transport him to an old folks' home in Salt Lake City before getting on with the rest of my life? And the little annoying voice keeps echoing in my head, "Levi, what are you doing? Why are you here?"

I've got to be honest. I'm not gonna lie. I am not doing this for pure reasons, the need to assist a family member, the cry of help by a dear loved one. I am not doing it because I am a necessarily good person or kind or caring or just about any other of those Boy Scout law things. I am doing it for a simple, basic, and probably base reason: money. I need the money.

Allow me to explain.

Allow me to tell you.

Allow me my youth, my greed, my pitiful finances, and my mounting bills.

Allow me those things, and maybe you will have a bit of sympathy for me and not quite write me off as purely mercenary or just some kind of immature tool. I have a story to tell.

I was at home, finishing up a summer as a boxboy and bagger in a grocery store. Me, a senior in college, and that was the best I could do, stuff frozen dinners and asparagus into bags. My friends had the hookups and good jobs that tied into what they wanted to do for the next thirty years of their lives. Clerking at a law office. An internship with a big accounting firm. An assistant account representative at a public relations outfit. I wanted to run from the room screaming whenever I heard what kind of jobs they lined up. It hurt. I couldn't brag because I had nothing to brag about. I needed a job, I needed money, and that's why I ended up saying about two hundred times a day, "Will that be paper or plastic, ma'am?"

I had no connections. Zero. My father owns a small photography studio and is hardly a titan of commerce. My boxboy duties called me back from my daydreaming: "Can I help you to the car? Can I get that door for you? Oh, that's quite all right—we have kids getting sick all the time in the store. It's just nature's way of saying, 'No thanks, stomach's not quite ready for that,' and I'll just get the mop and bucket and hustle right on down to aisle four. Don't you worry. We hope little Junior feels better. Cute little fellow, he is."

Don't get me wrong. Dad takes magnificent photos. He makes people *really* happy, and his handiwork is on display at hundreds of homes in our city, right over their fireplaces. He's a pure artist and a good technician and a lousy businessman, and he makes ends meet. We've lived in the same house for twenty-five years and will never move out or move up, we'll never want for family photos, and our Christmas cards are gorgeous.

Get the picture? That's my life.

But back to the original question. Why me, why am I in North Dakota, and why am I questioning the spherical relevance of the planet I call home?

Again, my answer: money. I like the stuff. I need it. Cash. Greenbacks. Bucks. Lincolns, Grants, and Franklins. *Dinero.*

It's like this: My aunt Barbara called one evening and chatted with my mother, just as I arrived home with my boxboy apron still hung around my neck. I faintly became aware that the conversation had moved on from the oh-hi-how-you-doing, how're-the–kids, and is-Gene-still-taking-pictures tone and seemed to be heading in my direction. It was not hard to pick up the clues.

"Oh yes, he's going back to school in a couple of weeks. No, not doing much. Bagging groceries. I think he's bored. It hasn't been much of a summer for him, I'm sure. No girlfriends, at least that we know of."

My ears began to burn. I ripped off my wretched grocery apron. I'd cleaned up two aisles that day.

"Oh yes, I'm sure he remembers Loyal. Down in Utah County that time. In the park. In the canyon. Such a sweet man."

Loyal? Uncle Loyal? Yes, I did remember him, but barely. I couldn't have been more than ten years old. Uncle Loyal and his wife, the one with the flower name—Rose, Pansy, Tulip, no, Daisy. That was it. They were there. Quiet people. Uncle Loyal sat on a small camp stool and hardly moved the whole time. Round face, big honkin' eyebrows, that's all I remembered about him. He looked like this really nice old guy. Good thing he wore the name tag. I wouldn't have known who he was.

Aunt Daisy was there next to them, and they sat and watched and held hands and smiled, and that was about it. Sweet people, I guess. They were from some third world country, one of those places you can see on a map but you're not sure really exists. North Dakota or Manitoba or Monrovia or someplace that sounded flat, cold, and boring. But about them? I didn't remember a lot.

Mother motioned me toward the phone. "It's Barbara, and she wants to talk with you, Levi. She has an idea that she wants to discuss with you."

Aunt Barbara is an interesting woman. There are things I admire about her. One. She is rich, loaded, wealthy beyond the comprehension of my feeble imagination. She married my mother's brother, Warren, and while Warren will never be mistaken for Warren Buffet or Donald Trump, he got in on the ground level of some kind of vacation-and-condo partnership exchange about fifteen years ago, which, near as I can tell, is a glorified pyramid scheme that caters to people who have too much money and need to find new places and ways to spend it so that they have all new fodder for their next family Christmas letter.

My guess is that Aunt Barbara is the go-to gal in the business, the brains that keeps it in the black, the oil in the money machine that lets it purr and hum. She has presence. She can be sneaky. She has a certain kind of latter-day chutzpah. She's a bit on the large side, wears her bleached blonde hair big, and jangles wherever she goes due to the approximately nineteen pounds of jewelry hanging from her wrists and neck at all times. She is a woman whom I'd call formidable, the kind of person who commands, demands, and gets respect. I want her as a friend, not as an unfriend.

Memo to Aunt Barbara: You have a bright, adorable nephew named Levi who is going to graduate with a business degree in the next year. Hint: He needs a job. Hint number two: Why not keep your business all in the family? I can book people to condos in Costa Rica.

Don't mistake her for a bad person. She's not. I think she has the grace and will to do some good things with her money, and she has the proverbial heart of gold right under all that jewelry. And, as I was about to learn, it is the combination of a good heart, her desire to have her father a little closer than North Dakota, and her willingness to depart with a few bucks that had me reaching for the phone, curious about what scheme my aunt had in mind for me.

"Levi, Barbara here. How is the grocery business this summer?" she asks.

"In the bag, Aunt Barbara, I've got it in the bag."

"Levi, that was awful. Simply awful. You should apologize."

"I should. It was. I couldn't help myself. I'm sorry."

"How much longer before you go back to school?"

"Two weeks. A little less."

"Your senior year, right?"

"Yep. Then it's off to see what life is all about. Places to go. People to see. Impressions to make. Upward and onward. I'm going to make a dent in this world."

"I have no doubt that it will be a large one. A very large dent. You have good skills."

I was thinking that Barbara was my favorite aunt. I could hear clinking and chinking as she moved the phone from one ear to the other and her baubles and bracelets flopped around. I could picture the light bouncing off her bleached blonde hair, sort of like a sunset over a big lake.

"I have a business proposition. Would you like to earn a little pocket change? I have something in mind." She paused, and then she said slyly, "I'd make it worth your time."

I liked those words. *I liked them very much.* Worth my time. Speak on, Aunt Barbara.

"I'm interested. Anything to boost my meager checking account. What were you thinking about?"

"It's my father, Loyal Wing. He lives in North Dakota, alone now. My mother died a long time ago, and I worry about my dad and the awful winters and being far from us. I want to bring him to the valley to live, but it's not as easy as putting him on a plane and getting him here. He doesn't like to fly. And he has some things that I know he'd like to take with him that he couldn't get on an airplane. And he likes to drive. He *absolutely loves* to be chauffeured. He'd just rather drive and look out the window and watch things go by than get in a plane and zip here in three hours. He's a quiet man but a perfectly *lovely* man."

Okay, I was thinking, so what did this have to do with me?

"He has agreed to come and live here in an assisted living home, but we need to get him to Utah. He lives in North Dakota, where I grew up. Did I already say that?"

This was becoming clearer. She said something about pocket change. Talk on, Lady Barbara. Speak to my heart, with words bracketed by dollar signs. Speak to me!

"I was wondering if you could get away from the grocery store, although I am sure they would miss you there because I am also sure that you are an excellent employee. I wondered if we flew you to North Dakota and rented a car, if you could drive the two of you to Utah."

The punch line. I was about to become a chauffeur, a driver for hire. But what about the bottom line? My bottom line, to be exact. I thought, *Minimum of three hundred, plus expenses.* She must have shifted the phone again from one ear to the other because the clatter of two armfuls of jewelry came tinkling over the phone.

"Of course, we'd pick up *all* the expenses, *absolutely.* The plane ticket, the car, money for food, and we could pay you five hundred dollars for your time and driving my father back."

My mind whirred with giddy delight. Five hundred dollars! Let's see, at my paltry boxboy wage, times forty hours, take away a little tax and the kick-in for the union dues, and cha-ching, I'd get to see beautiful North Dakota and take home *more than twice* what I would earn in the employ of the gigantic grocery store chain where they treat cans of tomato soup better than me. All of this was zinging through my head, and I was about ready to say, "Deal!" But Barbara, mistaking for reluctance the silence that accompanies my quick calculations, chipped in, "I know it's a *sacrifice*, Levi, and you would probably rather spend the last weeks of your summer with your family. Would six hundred dollars be fair compensation for your time and labor?"

Fair? Yes, more than fair. Twice as fair as what I had in mind. This is a deal. This is easy money. Take a flight, pick up the uncle unit, and then bomb back to Salt Lake City in record time, and I'll have six hundred bucks in my pocket. For six hundred smackers, I'd go pick up Attila the Hun on an elephant in the Alps.

I was coy enough to speak slowly. "I *was* hoping to spend time with my family because family comes first and we are close, as you know, but I think I can help you, Aunt Barbara. And I'd like to help your father out, because he's family too. You bet I remember him. Uncle Lewis. A great man, an idol to me. Yes, Uncle Lewis. What a sweet guy."

Uncle Lewis, no, Lawrence, no, Loyal. Loyal, Levi, not Lewis or Lawrence. Tall or short? Bald or full-head of hair? Thin or round? I was clouding up. Bald. Camp stool. Quiet. Them's the basics. And arched, bushy eyebrows that framed his face into a kind of triangle.

I heard Barbara clear her throat, and then her smooth, deep voice came flowing across the phone line. "Then let's put the plans together. Do you think you can make the trip next week?" She must have been happy because I heard clinking from her arms, her ears, her neck, and maybe even her toes. It was a happy clinking, I thought.

"I guess so. I'll check my calendar. Next week."

And so we made the plans. It was all quite simple, really. Just what she described. Fly to Bismarck, rent a car, pick up Uncle Loyal, and then zip him to the promised land. North Dakota. Is that where the place is where all the presidents have their faces carved into rock? Maybe we can take a little side trip. This is too easy. *Way too easy.* Pass go and collect my six hundred. I am The Road Warrior. I had worn the green grocer's apron for the last time. I gave notice the next day at the giant grocery conglomerate of which I someday hope to be the CEO.

That's the way it started, and how I came to blast across this dry, flat land on my way to pick up Uncle Loyal. It was as simple as that: a series of remarkable coincidences. Right place, right time, punch out of the grocery store, and set out on a most profitable and satisfying journey. Six hundred bucks! Whoa!

Let me make the noise one more time. *Cha-ching!*

I think Loyal is already becoming my favorite uncle.

CHAPTER THREE

HE COMES FOR ME
IN A VERY FAST RED CAR

I SAT ON THE FRONT steps of my home for only a quarter of an hour. I know what time my great-nephew arrived at the airport. I added in a little time to arrange for a car and then another two hours to make the drive to my old brown house. I assume he will drive fast across the flat land. There is a rhythm and cadence to life on the plains, and I have lived here long enough to understand it and the way it influences the comings and goings of people.

Levi, I am certain, will drive fast across the plains. He will think them ordinary. He likely knows no better.

What is there to do? Everything is packed, sent off, or sold. I taped a note to the front door for the new owners of the house—welcoming them, telling them it is a wonderful home. I understand they are a young couple. He has a sales route that takes him to the farms around this part of the state. They came from Wisconsin. They have two young children. I think my house will enjoy the young voices, the scuffling, the laughter, the joy of a cold Christmas morning when bright paper is sheared from gifts with abandon.

Across the street, Harriet Van Acker peers at me from her window. We have been neighbors for more than three decades. She lost her husband, Carl, six years ago. She waves to me shyly. She will not come out and bid me farewell. She did so a few days back, packing with her warm sweet rolls and a photo of Carl and me from many years ago, standing stiff as toy soldiers in front of my house. I cannot recall the occasion, why the photograph was snapped. Maybe there was no special occasion, just that we were there and someone had a camera. I am glad for the picture now. Carl was a good man and a good neighbor.

We have relied on each other, Harriet and I. Not in large ways, not in tangible ways. But we both knew the other was there and that we had the shared experience of losing a spouse. At times, that knowledge alone was helpful. Neither of us was quite alone in what we thought and felt and remembered.

"I will not come over to say good-bye," Harriet told me, her words sharp and chippy. "With Carl gone, and you leaving, and with Daisy and all. I feel alone now. Do you know? Yes, you must know. You feel it too." She lifted her hands, palms up, almost in an act of supplication. Then she dropped her hands to her sides. There is nothing to be done. She knows I am leaving.

"Tell me what it is like when you get there. Take care, Loyal, take care of yourself and come and visit if you can." She hands me the pan of sweet rolls and turns to leave. Over her shoulder, she says, "I will not come back. I will not. Don't even try to get me to."

She is a short, stout woman with gray glasses and gray hair. She wore an old blue dress, walking shoes, white socks, and despite the heat, a button-up sweater, top button clasped. She walked briskly back across the street to her home.

"Good-bye, Harriet. Good-bye and thanks. All will be well. I will tell you about Utah."

She turned and said, "I won't come back. I won't say good-bye to you, Loyal Wing." She resumed her pace and again spoke, straight ahead, words in a stiff line, "I hope the people who bought your home won't mind looking in on an old woman."

And those are the last words I heard from my neighbor.

But now, as I sit on my front porch, she looks at me from her window. I hold a hand up in acknowledgment. She waves a gallant hand back and then turns away.

I look toward the west from my front porch. Tall thunderheads tower, their anvil tops the shade and texture of cauliflower, and tens of thousands of feet below, their tails steel gray. A rain line drips from their fuzzy base.

Then I hear it, then I see it. Jagged lightning and the crack of thunder and the roar of an engine. My great-nephew Levi, it must be, announced by a magnificent thunderstorm.

A car, a very red car, driving too fast for our quiet street, turns the corner two blocks away. It is a car too new and too red for anyone in our town to drive. We are conservative in things of that nature. The driver is in a hurry, as most young people now seem to be.

I can see the driver, a young man, light brown hair, no longer a towhead. He is peering at addresses, looking to the right, then the left, then back to the right. He looks down at what I presume is a slip of paper with my address on it.

He sees me. He nods his head, gives me a half smile. He raises a hand in the air and gives me a wan wave, nothing like Harriet's stout farewell. Yes, this is my Levi, come to take me away, come to lead me home.

The car stops and he stretches before opening the door.

I wonder how much Barbara is paying him.

It looks as though I will be carried to my future in a red car that can be driven very fast.

I lift my suitcases and walk toward the car as Levi comes around the front and says, half-questioning, half-greeting, "Uncle Loyal?"

I do not look back at my brown house.

Across the street, Harriet Van Acker again waves forlornly and weeps like a child.

CHAPTER FOUR

THE DRONE OF A CAR ON THE ROAD MAY BE MY SALVATION

I DON'T KNOW WHAT I was looking for in Uncle Loyal. Just some old guy in a lime-green jumpsuit and shoes with Velcro. Maybe that was it. I hoped, and I don't want to sound unkind here, but I hoped he was mostly *with it*. Mentally, and I think you understand. Barbara hadn't said anything about him, you know, *slipping*. I hoped his gears still meshed.

"He's a sweet man. You'll love him" is about all she said. "Everyone loves him. He was a pharmacist. Forever. He knows everyone and everything in that town, right down to who has bunions. Everyone in that county and probably the next two over." I didn't have any more of a scouting report than that. Not much to go on.

Maybe he'd sleep all the way or most of the way like so many of the other older guys at church. He hears the drone of the highway and, boom, he's in dreamland. Drone of the highway, drone of a church speaker, about the same thing with the same results. The monotony of the scenery, the monotony of wheels on asphalt. *Monotony could be my salvation.* Suddenly, monotony is my friend. I'm pulling for monotony, which should come easily in this flat and plain land. My original plan still seems as though it will work. I'll blast across North Dakota, bomb through Montana, turn left toward Yellowstone, cut across the boot heel of Idaho, and then catch good old Interstate 80 and follow the Wasatch Front all the way to Bountiful. *Home in a flash.* I could be in Aunt Barbara's front yard by this time tomorrow night, maybe the following morning. It would mean driving almost straight through. But I could get a few winks here and there at a rest stop if I need it, slosh down fizzy energy drinks, then peel back the eyelids and hit the road again. *This is too easy.* Six hundred dollars!

Me and the road. We are one. And the hot red car. We are one. Uncle Loyal and me, we are not one. Please, as long as he isn't in a jumpsuit, as long as he has most of his marbles, as long as he can take care of himself.

As long as he doesn't have the old-guy smell. Please. Anything else I can handle for twenty-four hours.

Steel yourself, Levi. You can do this. You passed business calc. This is a business proposition. Even Aunt Barbara used that word: *proposition*. She knows. A contract. She has a business need; I have the means to fulfill it. That's what America is all about. That's what free enterprise is all about. Make a buck by helping each other out. *That's* the American way. *That's* what I'm all about. An agreement to take care of a transaction that meets mutual needs. I remember something like that from an entry-level business class textbook. A man of business, that's what I am, and I'm about ready to pocket a tidy profit for fairly easy duty.

Six hundred bucks! Did I mention I'll earn six hundred dollars for about one long day's worth of work? What does Barbara think I am? A doctor? A lawyer? A plumber?

She said if we decided to stay over somewhere to just put it on the shiny yellow credit card that she handed to me at the airport. I don't know. I'd rather just head straight from here to there and not have to worry about being roommates with an old guy. That might be a little too weird for me, the old-man talk, the old-man wheezing, the old-man habits. On the other hand, I suppose we could get separate rooms. I could order room service, a dream of mine. Big, greasy, meaty, cheesy pizza. I could get a room with a balcony and a view and watch sports all night long and take a dip in the pool. Why not? *Someone else is paying the freight, Levi.*

Now, to find his place. Brown house, even numbered, must be on the right side of the street. All the houses look pretty much the same. Welcome to Small Town, North Dakota, where the checker game at the fillin' station every Saturday night is the biggest show around. Every other house, I bet, has a Sven, a Lars, or an Ole in it.

I think I see the house.

And that must be Uncle Loyal. He looks vaguely familiar. He fits the description: old, white male, monster eyebrows, sitting in front of a house with a sold sign in front, two suitcases and two big boxes. All that is missing is a little sign that says, "Utah or bust."

And no jumpsuit. Life is good. I love being an American and earning a buck the old-fashioned way. *Easy. Quick. Not much to it.*

No doubt. This is the place. I've spotted my quarry.

I get out of my car and I call him by name. He nods and moves toward me, carrying one of the old suitcases and a small brown paper bag under one arm. He leaves a suitcase and the two large boxes on the porch.

He looks like a little old owl. "Levi. My pleasure to meet you once more," he says. He speaks in a formal way, draws out the vowels. Must be sort of a plains accent. And he tosses in an occasional "eh" at the end of a sentence. Local color, local speech pattern, I suppose.

Levi, your ship has come in. And he's not wearing a jumpsuit. Did I mention that?

If I hustle, we can make four hundred miles before midnight.

This is so darned easy.

It's time to get down to business.

CHAPTER FIVE
IN THE RED CAR,
WE MEET THE ANVIL CLOUDS OF ZEUS

MY NEPHEW LOOKS AT ME curiously. He doesn't know who I am, what to make of me. I hope he is a nice young man who doesn't mind spending a few days with a nice old man.

"Loyal? Loyal Wing?" he calls. "Uncle Loyal?" His gaze shifts from side to side, quickly, nervously. He seems in a hurry, which is something I am unaccustomed to. Here on the plains, men my age, we move slowly. We move deliberately, a purpose to our motion. I wonder if most young men of the next generation are like Levi, and I conclude they probably are. They have yet to recognize the beauty of slowness.

"I am Loyal. You must be Levi, my great-nephew, eh? We met once before, a few years back in a lovely canyon with a stream running through it. I thank you for coming. Your grace is appreciated. There must be many other things you'd rather be doing than taking a distant relative to Utah."

He shuffles his feet a bit and says, no, this is what he wants to be doing, it was all fine, it was all good.

"Do you have any other suitcases? Anything I can give you a hand with? There's still some daylight left, quite a lot, I'd say, although I'm not sure when the sun sets here in Minnesota."

"North Dakota," I remind him.

"Whatever. One of those states in the middle and toward the top. Anyway, I thought we could get on the road and head out, maybe make a few hundred miles yet tonight. Or we could just drive until I get tired. But I don't get tired much when I'm behind the wheel," he says.

I purposely do not look behind me at my old house. "Yes. We could. There is no purpose in me staying here longer. This part is over for me. It might prove more difficult for me to linger. As you said, we could put some mileage behind us. I suppose there isn't much of a reason to stay here, no reason to prolong what must be done. We may as well go."

But my will fails me. This time, I cannot resist the call to turn around and look at the old brown house once more. In my heart, I say good-bye to the house, to the memories, to my girls when they were little, to Daisy, to the blizzards of the plains, to the draining July heat. I say good-bye to sprinkling my lawn, hose in hand, on those summer evenings, the gentle hissing of the water pouring forth, the random thoughts floating pleasantly through my mind after a long day. Yes, I could have solved any problem in the world at those times, with the heat of the day over, the hose gently vibrating, and time to think the thoughts that came naturally. I say good-bye to the big front porch, to each tree I had planted, to the big-headed sunflowers in my yard, to each shrub I had tenderly placed in the good plains soil. I say good-bye to the azure spring sky of North Dakota, the violent black sky just before a late-summer thunderstorm sweeps in. I say all of those good-byes in mere seconds, look at my feet, heft one of my suitcases, then watch as Levi walks back to the porch for the remaining boxes and suitcase. And then I follow Levi around to the trunk of the car.

He pushes a button on his key chain, and the trunk opens. He reaches for my suitcases, lifts them inside, and slaps the trunk closed. He puts my boxes in the backseat, rubs his hands, and says, "I guess that's it. Time to go. Seems like a nice place, very North Dakota, if you know what I mean. Quaint. And flat, and if I say so, hot. Really hot today. You've lived here awhile. Aunt Barbara said so."

"Yes, awhile. A long time, really. Maybe too long."

"Bet it's tough to leave. Aunt Barbara said you know everyone."

"Almost. Except for a handful of the newer families. They're the only ones I'm not acquainted with. Just the new families. They go to the new pharmacy in the big store in Grand Forks. The others I know. I helped nurse many of them through difficult circumstances. Talking with a young and rattled mother about her child's wheezing on a subzero January night. Or soothing the itch of a child who found the poison oak patch. You learn the most about people when they face difficult circumstances."

"Oh yeah. Bet you do. And I know what you mean about people all heading toward the new big stores. Little markets, big markets. Those big-box stores, it's tough to compete with them. You see, I know something about all this. I'm a business major. I'm going to get my degree next spring. But those big stores. Drove a lot of little businesses under." He jangles his keys and tosses his head in the general direction of the car. He wants to be on the way; patience does not appear to be a characteristic of my young great-nephew. "Well, I guess we can go now."

"Yes. Let's go. There's no need to stay longer. No need to idle."

"Okay."

He looks around, up and down the street, then walks to the driver's side of the car, opens the door, and half beckons me to join him. I get in the car and adjust my seat belt. The car smells all at once new, fresh, leathery, and oily. Levi starts the engine, which first roars and then purrs. He pushes the gas pedal again and grins when he hears the satisfying rev from under the hood. He jerks the car into gear, and with a lurch, we move forward.

I wonder what Daisy would think of all this, my grand exit from our home, our town, among the last tangible links to our intertwined life. Leaving in a sporty red car, leaving late in the afternoon, leaving with a nephew I don't really know for a place I don't know at all. I hope that from somewhere in the expanse of the kingdom of God, she looks upon me kindly, lovingly, and says, "Dear, sweet Loyal, it will all be right, you will be fine, and someday, in a time so short that it will seem to you a blink of the eye, we will be reunited."

I like to think these kind of thoughts, what she would say, the kind instruction she would give, at the times when I am lonely. She knows more than I do at this point. I hope a kind God allows her to peer through portals to earth when I need an unseen uplifting hand. I think He does. He must care for the lonely. They must have special dispensation with Him.

And now, even in the company of my great-nephew Levi, with a new part of life just ahead of me, I am, indeed, lonely, and if a man my age can be frightened, I am that, too. But I must not show it. If you feel it and then show it, you will act it, and it will come to be. I can do little about my feelings. But I must stop them before showing them. The plains have imbued me with stoicism and independence and a way to deal with unwanted change and a heart that trembles.

We drive away from my house, away from my street. Levi reaches the main street of our town and asks which way we turn.

"To the left. That's west, the way we need to go," I tell him. I feel a little of what the pioneers must have experienced, leaving a home, looking west, moving toward a setting sun, and for some, with dark clouds hugging the horizon. Levi guns the engine again as we turn onto the highway, and we lurch forward. This is my life passing before me, at forty-five miles an hour in a twenty-five-mile zone.

I should have guessed we would drive by my old pharmacy, made of stone, graceful in its age. Driving by must have been a part of a grander scheme of things. It gives me a chance to say good-bye again. A gift boutique, its windows filled with dry flowers and homemade wood boxes and frames, occupies it now. Soon we are beyond the edge of the city, and the great fields of grain stretch to the horizon. Above, the black clouds loom, and Zeus hurls his crooked bolts of lightning to the ground, and the rumbling of thunder gurgles our way from the center of the storm. Levi seems not to notice.

The plains are beautiful at times such as these. Subtle as a wheat stalk, bold as forked lightning splintering a tree.

I wonder what kind of sign this is, the lightning and the thunder, if any kind of sign at all. Daisy used to say that I saw too many signs in too many things.

I stare straight ahead. I can't look at this road, the fields, the houses that sit like wooden ships on a golden ocean, anymore. I can't look at the names on the mailboxes. I know these people. I love these people. Levi reaches for the radio, flips it on, and pushes the scan button.

"Do you have any decent radio stations out here?" he asks. "I'm not really into country, if you know what I mean. But almost anything else. Except jazz. And classical. But everything else is okay. Not oldies, though. I should have brought some of my own music. Forgot to. I can't believe I forgot."

He makes a face toward the radio, his frustration obvious. Ahead, lightning splits the evening air, and in the distance I see the majestic sweep of a rain line.

I think this will be a strong storm. The makings are all in place. Shall I take it as a salute from nature at my departure? Lightning forks a crooked hand across the sky, and the thunder rattles through the din of the fast red car bolting down the two lanes of asphalt.

As we whip past the signs and markers, the fences and tall stalks of grain, we hurtle our way toward the westward horizon.

Levi shoots me a quick glance, smiles impishly, and says, "Don't worry, Uncle Loyal. I'll have us in Utah before you know it."

Chapter Six

He Says We Might Be Near a Tornado and Then Hands Me a Ham Sandwich

THE CLOUDS AHEAD, THEY'RE DARK. Really dark. I can see lightning shooting out of them every so often. I wonder, *Should we be heading right into this storm? What do you do in these North Dakota boomers? Pull over? Drive ahead? Find a bed and crawl under the blankets? Whimper? I don't know. Should I ask Uncle Loyal?*

I've seen some good thunderstorms in my day, but this one has them all beat. I switch on my headlights. I look at the speedometer, and we're doing eighty-five. I ease up a little. A bolt smashes down, maybe a quarter of a mile away. Even over the engine's roar, the thunder booms and sends a shiver through the car. It's starting to rain. It's starting to hail. The end is near! I expect to see a funny old guy dressed in white with a long scraggly beard with a sign announcing that the world is about to be swallowed up whole. This seems apocalyptic. Biblical. Just plain ugly. I push a knob, and the windshield wipers are flipping full speed back and forth. I sneak a glance at Uncle Loyal. I can't read him. His face is glassy. He's just staring straight ahead. He seemed fairly normal back at the house, but now, not so much. Ignoring this storm is like ignoring that you're going through a car wash. With your windows down. Only this is louder. I get this vision in my mind of an old movie. I used to have nightmares about tornadoes after watching *The Wizard of Oz*. We might be the local version of Dorothy and Toto, for all I know. But Uncle Loyal just keeps his eyes on the road. Maybe this isn't a big deal to him, just a gentle North Dakota summer shower, good for rinsing the dust out of the air.

Uncle Loyal looks at me and says pleasantly, "Big storm, eh?"

Lightning jags down maybe a couple of hundred yards away, and the instant roar causes my stomach to knot up. My hands are locked on the steering wheel with a viselike grip. Finally, I crack, and my voice comes out squeaky, a little-boy croak, the same kind of sound I made when my upper lip first turned fuzzy.

"Is this normal, Uncle Loyal? The lightning seems to be hitting awfully close."

He looks toward me and gives me a thin smile and says, "Oh, this is a pretty good one. Pretty good indeed. We get one of these every week or two this time of the year. But I don't think there are any tornadoes associated with it. We should not be fearful."

Tornadoes? He said tornadoes. That is a word that sends big alarms off in me. That is not the word I wanted to hear. Next stop: Munchkin Land. I may die in North Dakota.

Stay calm, Levi. Don't squeal or flutter or panic or let your eyes bug out too far. You were a Star Scout. You earned eight merit badges and one of them was meteorology, I think. Another was first aid. Both of them might come in handy. I mentally review the steps for artificial resuscitation. *Tilt the head back and thump the chest. Or is it the other way around?* Every news report I've ever seen with a reporter standing grim-faced and nothing but twisted metal and broken trees in the background flashes across my mind. "This is where the town of Bumperbelt, North Dakota, stood until last night," the reporter says, nodding over his shoulder toward the remains of a red car. "These travelers, a brilliant and handsome young man in the flower of life and his older companion never knew what hit them. Now, they are like day-old bacon."

In the most calm voice I can muster, I ask a question, but my voice still comes out about the way it did when I was thirteen years old: up and down, up and down, and cracking.

"Tornado! Could we be in a tornado? What should we do? Hide under the car?" Well, that didn't quite come out right.

I drop my speed all the way down to sixty. I'm having a hard time seeing the road ahead.

Uncle Loyal looks outside for a moment. He scans the sky and ever so mildly says, "No, I don't believe any tornadoes are touching down. There's no green in the sky, and when a tornado is close, the sky takes on a green tint. Odd, but it does. I've seen plenty of tornadoes in my day, but this sky doesn't quite look right for one."

The hail pounds, and my wipers are almost useless. I worry that the car might get dented and the rental company will hold me responsible. Aunt Barbara might not enjoy getting the bill for a totaled car, done in by hail the size of golf balls.

I nod my head. For some reason, maybe to show that I am cool and calm and in control, and not scared out of my wits, I start to whistle.

"Are you nervous, Levi?" Uncle Loyal looks at me sweetly, the way a parent would ask, "And how was your spelling test this afternoon, Junior?"

"No, no. Me, nervous? Nope. Ha! Well, maybe a little. You said a word that caught my attention, though." I glanced and him and lowered my voice. " Tornado."

"I think we'll be fine. You need not worry."

The hail pounds the car. I wish I had read the fine print of the rental contract to know if I will be responsible for dents caused by Mother Nature. How will I tell Aunt Barbara? Guess what? I not only got your father to Utah but as a bonus, I bought you a new car in the process! *Insurance.* I hope the rental company has insurance. My mind wraps around the word and clings to it, the way a drowning man clings to a chunk of wood from a shipwreck.

I can't see more than twenty feet ahead, and the dark gray veil is growing thicker. I slow to maybe forty miles an hour. Is it my imagination, or is the sky looking faintly green?

"Do you think we should pull over?"

"There isn't much visibility."

"I can't stop on the highway."

"If you drive another quarter mile, you'll see a large white mailbox. Just beyond it is a wide driveway that leads to a farmhouse. It's John Jannuzzi's place. We can pull into the drive and wait out the storm. These storms usually don't last more than an hour or so."

I do not know John Jannuzzi, but I love the man, and I love that he's a friend of Uncle Loyal and that he owns a house only a quarter mile away.

"Will it be okay if we pull off there? Is there a chance John what's-his-name will run into us?"

"No, Levi." Uncle Loyal smiles, a wispy little grin, and his eyebrows lift up and form that odd triangle on his forehead. "John's lived on the prairie his whole life. He knows better than to come out in this kind of weather. He probably saw this cloudburst coming more than an hour ago. He knows the plains and how the weather works here. And it's common to borrow a road or driveway to wait out a storm. It's customary. It's neighborly."

I slow again and hope nobody behind is coming fast toward us. Maybe Uncle Loyal is right. The natives understand this weather, and they stay at home when they see the dark clouds gathering, sort of a local native custom, like when chickens stop laying eggs just before an earthquake. At this moment, I am really, really glad to have grown up in Utah and not

North Dakota or South Dakota or Iowa or Nova Scotia or any place that has tornadoes.

I keep my eyes peeled for the mailbox. Out of the gloom, between the sheets of drenching rain and pounding hail, it appears, shimmering for a burst of a second when the wiper blades swish across the windshield.

"Here?"

"Yes. Turn here. If you'd like, we could probably drive right to John's house. He'd let us in, and we could wait out the storm."

"Let's see what happens. Let's just sit it out in the car, if we can."

I bring the car to a stop, scrunching as close as I can to the side of the broad, gravel driveway. Outside, lightning crackles, thunder booms, and rain slashes at the side of the car. It's dark; it's gloomy. The car sways a little when the wind gusts.

It's all kind of creepy. I begin to feel queasy. The wind howls. The hail beats against the car. I'm stuck somewhere on the plains of North Dakota sitting next to someone I barely know, a long road ahead of me. The six hundred dollars? I may be earning it after all.

Where am I? What am I doing here? Tell me again. Someone. I need assurance. I need comfort. I need someone to tell me it will be all right. I need my night light.

Uncle Loyal looks down on the floor and picks up the paper bag that he carried into the car with him. He reaches inside and pulls out what looks to be food in the dim evening light.

"Are you hungry?" he asks. "This is what I thought. I thought you might be in a hurry, you might want to start our trip tonight. I thought if I made some sandwiches, it could save us time. I made them at the house; I cleared out the last of my food this afternoon. I left the refrigerator for the new couple. I won't need it in Utah."

He calmly pushes the sandwich in my direction. You'd think we were on a picnic, not hiding out from a monster storm. Lightning forks down, illuminating his face. I manage a quick glance at him. He looks gentle, serene, sweet. In the middle of a storm, with tornadoes possibly swirling across the land waiting to sweep us away and whirl us into a dark and chaotic world, Uncle Loyal is at ease with himself, his surroundings, and quite possibly, his life. *A tornado couldn't move him.* It all comes to me in a flash. A literal flash, as the lightning strikes again.

This is a man who is sure of himself and sure of his element. Calm radiates from him. Calmness is contagious. I clear my throat. I look out the window. Suddenly, I feel much more at ease.

I think Loyal Wing might be a man worth knowing because he understands how to ride out storms. That has to be high on anyone's list of skills.

"Eh?" he asks gently. "They should be good sandwiches. Made with bread baked by my neighbor, Harriet Van Acker."

Suddenly, I feel hungry, and a sandwich sounds just right. Comfort food, and believe me, I need comfort.

"Sure. Thanks. I am hungry. I haven't eaten anything since breakfast, and that was a fast-food, greasy plastic-like egg substance wrapped around mystery meat in a tortilla. You know, I got kind of caught up in everything, the travel here, trying to get some miles behind me. I was in a hurry and forgot to eat. Not my brightest move."

"It's easy to do. Trying to put some miles behind you. We're all guilty of that at times." He hands me the sandwich, thick with ham and veggies, on a grainy wheat bread.

"Ham and cheese and vegetables," he says. "The lettuce and tomatoes are from my garden. Or rather, the garden I had. Mrs. Van Acker makes a very fine loaf of bread. Something I shall miss. "

I take the sandwich.

"Here. I brought some juice and water. Please, take something to drink."

The wind seems to let up some. The hail stops thumping and turns into a steady rain. The sky grows lighter, and I no longer worry about being smacked by a tornado. I feel a little embarrassed about how squeaky and fearful I had been. No munchkins, no witches in sight, and the worst of the storm seems to have blown over.

Uncle Loyal chews slowly on his sandwich. He is dressed in corduroy pants and a blue, long-sleeved shirt, buttoned to the top. He seems as calm as if he were watching flowers grow in his garden. Chew, chew, chew, swallow. Another bite, chew slowly and swallow. A day in the park, a day in the garden, a pleasant roadside stop for him.

At the peak of the storm, this man hands me a sandwich, offers me juice to drink, and my world is jerked from one side to another.

"Are you not hungry?"

I hadn't started on my sandwich.

"Yes, yes, I am. I'm sorry. I was daydreaming. I am very hungry. Thank you, Uncle Loyal. That was thoughtful of you." I bite into my sandwich, and yep, Harriet Van Whoever makes a stunningly good loaf of bread.

The sun is behind the last of the dark clouds to the west, the storm little more than a drizzle. A rainbow spins out of the sky, arching against the dark clouds, splashy and reassuring.

"I should tell you something, Levi. I have a confession." He stops chewing. He shifts toward me on the front seat of the car. He places his hands on his corduroy pants.

"What?"

"I *was* a trifle concerned about that storm. More than I let on. I've seen lots of storms like that, and tornadoes have been known to touch down from those kinds of clouds. But I didn't want you to worry," he says, pointing his chin upward a little. "No, I wouldn't want that."

"Since we're both into confessions, I have one for you. I *was* worried. I never did like *The Wizard of Oz*. I thought we might wake up with little giggly green people surrounding us."

"We might have. I wonder if that is what paradise is like. Eh?"

"Too early for me to find out."

"I agree. Too early for me as well. I'd like to add on a few more years. We have much ahead of us, Levi. Much to look forward to."

The sandwich is wonderful. I wash the last of it down with my fruit juice. The rain drips onto the car with a pleasing patter. Suddenly, I feel very tired. I have been up since four in the morning, traveled halfway across the country, met a distant relative named Loyal, packed the old fellow up, and then started back to Zion again. It has been a long day. *A very long day.* My thoughts get filmy and slow. My eyes close. It is nice to just see darkness and not crazy lightning bolts touching down. I think of a green witch and big monkeys with long tails that somehow can fly. Just for a second, I tell myself. I'll keep them closed only for a moment. Just for a second or two. Way off in the distance, I hear a now-gentle roll of thunder and the slow, polite munching on a ham-and-cheese sandwich.

Almost two hours later, I wake up. The night is warm and humid, and I can see by the stars winking in the sky that the storm is over.

Chapter Seven

In Poetry and Fable, Heading West Is Not Good

Levi fell asleep as the storm waned. I imagine he was tired. He said he had arisen at four, and he had traveled very far.

I am a patient man. Living on the prairie all these years, attending to people who were ill, running a business on my own, all that and more, has taught me patience. You learn first not to let your own concern come through in your voice, then not to frown, and then to smile when a baby has the croup and a young, frightened mother calls at three in the morning, panicked and seeking your help. You watch the seasons and wait for the burning heat of August to turn gradually to a cool autumn, then the gray, clipped afternoons of January, slowly, in tiny steps, giving way to the first pale green buds of spring. You learn to let this old earth turn on its hinges, and you realize you are a mere passenger. You learn to let things run their course. You come to understand time and its meanings. You learn there really isn't much difference between minutes and hours, days and weeks. When you do try to move things faster than their natural gait, it is all too easy to become frustrated and then disappointed. When you rush things, you may lose their meaning. I suppose God wants us to notice things and learn. I suppose He gives us experiences that we might sort through them, retain what we should, discard what we don't need, and inch along toward what we are destined to be in the eternities. Gods, yes; that is at the core of our belief; but even among the gods, there will, I believe, be distinctness, separateness, individuality.

Levi will learn patience too. Only in time, as patience must be learned. He will learn that even in a severe thunderstorm, with hail bashing down and lightning spitting, it is best to be patient, watchful, calm, and learn from it all.

These lofty and bold thoughts come to me as I wait and watch my great-nephew fall into a deep sleep behind the steering wheel of a fast red car, idled by a hot-breathed prairie storm that boomed across our path.

I believe he was truly frightened by the storm. It was a good one—oh, golly, but what a good one. Powerful, furious. And lovely. I think that, wherever heaven is, there will be storms because storms can be magnificent and possess a terrible and haunting beauty, and we learn more in storms than under fair skies. I suppose we need both.

When Levi was deep in slumber and the rain had turned to drizzle then the drizzle diminished to a fine spray, I quietly open the car door and slide outside. I take in the deep darkness of the night, the fragrance of rain on crops. I listen to the crickets courting. I wonder if I will hear crickets in my new Utah home. I wonder what the Utah air smelled like when a summer thunderstorm washed it clean.

I think about Daisy. She had been fascinated by the violent weather we so often saw in North Dakota. When the thunder rumbled like a freight train across the plains and the lightning came in wicked sheets and forks, she seldom retreated farther into the house but rather moved to the largest window we had and searched the skies for what would come next. I recall, during one early cold snap, when the temperatures dropped to ten below zero before November, coming home from work and seeing her in the front yard, clad in a light sweater, looking up in the darkness, her shape illuminated only by the pale yellow light on our porch.

I asked softly, "Why are you out here?"

She said, "To feel what it's like. The cold makes me feel alive." To feel.

On this August night, a quarter mile away, John Jannuzzi's home is awash in light. It is a lighted ship in a calm sea. The glow reaches out and invites me in. But I do not want to leave Levi. And I have said my good-byes to these people once and do not know if I could say good-bye to any of them again.

The wind comes from the west and whispers to me.

I close my eyes and try to remember what Utah is like. I remember mountains. Perhaps I will like the mountains, though I know little of them. I remember people. I remember them in their hurries.

I say Daisy's name in a muted voice, once more, and let the breeze carry my word across the prairie. The rustling of John's cornstalks seems to murmur her name back to me.

Inside the car, Levi rustles and mumbles something and then drifts deeper into sleep.

Cars speed by on the state highway we turned off an hour ago, their headlights like small fireflies at first, growing larger as they come to the intersection of John's driveway, the whooshing of their engines building momentum and then, after they pass by, quickly falling into nothingness. The air becomes still again. The chorus of crickets and rustling cornstalks plays a subdued, two-part harmony.

How did it come to this, I wonder. Is this decision, to move from my home to Utah, the right one? Is there a right decision at all? Does it matter to the Lord where I live out my final days? Have I lost my usefulness? I am old, but I still want to be needed.

I have been needed here, and that is part of what makes these prairies my home. Your home is where you feel needed.

There is a small branch in our town. On good Sundays, we have twenty-five people attend. Floyd McKay was the only other male experienced enough to be the branch president. So we rotated. Floyd would serve four or five years, and then he would get tired or discouraged or his wife would say enough, and he would ask for a release. The stake president would then call me in and ask me to serve. After four or five years, when I would get tired or discouraged or Daisy would hint that we had experienced enough on this round, I would talk to the stake president, and Floyd would be called in for another hitch. We each served as the branch president three times. Floyd is in his third year of his third turn. But he is also now old and I am leaving, and we do not know who will replace us.

It was much the same for Mary McKay and Daisy. It was not unusual for one of them to play the piano, the other to lead the singing. Then one would teach the Gospel Doctrine class and the other Relief Society. Mary bore a larger burden since Daisy died. Then she was the only person in our branch who played the piano. Such is the way with the Church away from Utah, from Idaho, from Arizona, and so many other places where it is well established. We make it work with what we have. We are needed.

But it is no longer mine to worry about. The Lord will provide for our branch. I hope a family or two moves our way. I hope our little branch isn't combined with the small ward thirty-five miles from our town. I hope a pianist comes to us. Or that someone volunteers to learn to play.

Outside the car, it is warm and damp, and the land seems alive, an unseen world of insects and small animals throbbing to a beat and rhythm only they can hear and feel.

To Utah. I will go to Utah and be surrounded by those of our faith. But is this all *right*? The question returns.

I will live among people more or less my age. I will form a few friendships. I will be closer to Barbara and Warren and their children, and other family members, too. I will be close to good medical care. In the mornings, I will look to the east and see the tall Wasatch peaks, as they are called, and watch them turn from shadows to mountains, from black to gray to blue.

And I will miss my house in North Dakota and the friendships that took me four decades to build. I have seen one generation, then another, and then a third spring from these plains, fresh faces, new hopes rising. They are things not easily replaced. To move is to close a door on one way of life and start over in another. Even when you are eighty-two years old. You can still start over. Sometimes you must start over. *Is it right?* I suppose the answer is you must make it right, Loyal. It is right to stay, right to leave, right to do whatever else. The choice is yours. Pencil out the sketch of your life, then fill it in with hard, fast colors that will not fade.

I can, with only faint imagination and in a voice not quite a whisper, hear Him: "Trouble me not, Loyal. You may choose, and you and I will go along about the same. You are eighty-two years old. Make your choice, and I will be with you, I will support you. I will leave you enough manna in the wilderness and water from a brook until you are able to sustain yourself."

In the distance, I hear a nighthawk's shrill cry. The moon rises and glows through filmy clouds. I hear cattle lowing from John Jannuzzi's barn. The soil, like the air, smells warm, moist, and pungent. *Alive.* The earth smells like the sky, and I hear the rustle of cornstalks and wonder if it is the whispering of angels.

Levi is fitful. He has slumped over on the car seat and is now almost in a prone position in the front seat. He sniffles in his sleep. He lets out a long sigh. My young nephew is restless.

Were I at home now, I would be lying down, the window open, a book in my hand. I would read, then listen, then read some more, and listen again. My television set broke five years ago. I never replaced it. I never missed it. I did not own a computer. I wrote all of my letters by hand, on big sheets of light brown paper. I sent out far more letters than I received, but I will continue writing them. It is part of the old way. Pen in hand, words to paper.

Levi mumbles something in his sleep, then coughs lightly. He smacks his lips and stretches an arm up toward the window. He soon will awake, and we will begin our journey again. To the west. To the mountains and valleys of Utah. To my new home.

I have read enough to know that in folklore and poetry, a traveler who moves west moves toward unhappiness. It is a symbol I must counter.

Levi sits up. He looks around, bewildered by his surroundings. He does not know where he is, what he is doing. Then he looks at me through the door, left half open.

"Uncle Loyal?"

"Levi."

"I must have fallen asleep. Let's see. I remember the storm and the farmhouse of your friend. Where are we again? What time is it? How long have I been asleep?"

"Awhile. You needed the rest. Shall we push on now?"

He seems to regain his senses and bearings. A thought seems to snap him awake.

"Sure. Yeah, let's get moving again."

He fishes the car keys out. Quietly, I climb back into the car. He turns the engine on and carefully backs down to the highway. This time, he doesn't need to ask me for directions. He turns the car to the left.

A barn owl blows three somber notes in the thick night air.

I take in a breath of fresh, soily air as the lights of John Jannuzzi's house fade into the night. I hear a noise, swishing, swooshing, like a murmur from beyond, and think that maybe angels are watching over me as the car tires crinkle over small gravel.

Levi turns the car to the west, and in mere seconds, we are again moving toward our destination.

CHAPTER EIGHT

DRIVE STRAIGHT LIKE AN ARROW

ALMOST TWO HOURS! HOW COULD I have slept that long in a car just after a tornado might have touched down and ripped me off the face of the planet? Uncle Loyal must have been awake the whole time. He didn't say a thing to me. Just let me sleep. Sandwiches first, then sleep. Eat, sleep, breathe. The basics of life. Uncle Loyal just sat there and let me do what I needed to keep the Levi organism functioning.

I will give him credit. Credit for watching out for me. There seems to be more to Uncle Loyal than meets the eye. Or at least my eye, untrained as it is. More than Aunt Barbara told me. More than Aunt Barbara *realizes*. He reminds me of some of the tribal elders I met on my mission in northern Arizona. They didn't say much. They just sat there and oozed wisdom and time and experience, and you got the feeling they'd *earned* each of their wrinkles. Sometimes they didn't say *anything*, but you felt different and better just by having been around them. I suppose wisdom never is loud and never draws attention to itself.

When I wake up, he's just standing outside the car, his head cocked slightly, listening and looking.

"Uncle Loyal?"

"Eh, Levi?"

"How long have I been asleep?"

"Awhile. An hour and one-half or so. But you needed it. The storm is over. We should be driving again. I know you're in a hurry to make good time."

"Okay."

He tilts his head upward. I see the moon, a little fuzzy, as if there are a bunch milky clouds in front of it. I look toward the east, where the sky is darker. I see stars. Lots of them. It is a peaceful, sweet feeling, almost as if the night sky is apologizing for the violence of the storm.

"Summer sky," he says, getting back into the car. "The summer constellations. You can see so many of them from here. Most people think you need to be on the top of a mountain to see the stars well. The view from the prairie is fine."

He plops down next to me. I start the engine, shaking out the cobwebs, eager to be on the road again to make up for lost time, if you ever really can do such a thing.

"Vega, Deneb, and Altair."

I thought he was speaking in tongues.

"Say what?"

"Vega, Deneb, and Altair. Three of the brightest stars in the summer sky. You must know of them, you must have heard of them. Legend says that Vega is part of the lyre that Apollo taught Orpheus to play. Orpheus learned the instrument so well that he could calm savage beasts with it. When Orpheus died, the harp continued to play. The gods put Vega in the sky to honor his music."

I couldn't think of much to say, since my knowledge of the stars equates roughly with my knowledge about how to knit a quilt. Or crochet. Or sew. Or whatever you do to make a quilt. But a lack of knowledge has never been something to stop me from speaking, so I sputter, "Yeah, Vega. I think it was named after a car. Nice story, the harp and all."

Then I say, "You must have read up a lot on it."

"Not so much reading, more looking. I like to look up. And I like to know what I see when I look up." He smiles again, as though he had told some kind of a deep and private joke. "I sometimes worry that I spend too much time looking down or to the side, Levi. We miss God's magnificent stars. We can learn more about ourselves when we look up. There's a pattern up there too. We miss too much. God works in patterns. I learned that a long time ago."

"Yeah, sure." Well, I knew *at that point* that He worked in patterns because Loyal had just told me.

We move ahead, down the two-lane blacktop, driving straight like an arrow that had been shot toward a target. I can see puddles on the side of the road. Bugs are starting to rise out of the fields and occasionally splat against the windshield. The keys in the ignition jangle pleasantly. Again, I think of my mission to Arizona and how, in some of my assignments, we drove long distances on warm summer nights. It all felt pleasant, it all felt *right* during those long trips through the desert, the shadows of sandstone cliffs and mountains outlined against the madrone and manzanita, dark against the fading midnight blue of the sky.

It was easy to think at those times, and it was easy to feel bigger than you really were.

We pass the lights of farmhouses. Each little farmhouse had a family, and each family had a story to tell, their own lives to lead, I think. The farmhouses look snug and secure, their yellow light splashing out into the night. I think how nice it would be after the storm to pull up in front of one of those homes, be greeted by a family, smacked on the back then, hand to shoulder, welcomed and invited in.

And the chances were Uncle Loyal knew the families who belonged to each farmhouse. The chances were, he *would* be smacked on the back, hands to his shoulders, and welcomed as a friend. It's what his life was about, what he had achieved, what he had *earned*.

And me. I wanted to be a man of business. Maybe the warm welcomes would come afterward. After I earned my millions, my fame, my spectacular home, my trophy wife and kids.

Man. Drive through a tornado, eat a good ham sandwich, sleep a little, and all of a sudden, I'm getting *philosophical*. Maybe it is the Dakota air.

But I have to admit something else as we blast down the highway. I had underestimated the man sitting next to me in the car. I'm starting to kind of like Uncle Loyal. People have underestimated me for much of my life—hey, I was bagging groceries just three days ago—and I shouldn't be so quick to judge someone else. Everyone has *something* to offer.

I let up on the accelerator. There is no reason to go so fast, especially at night. *Make these cool moments last, Levi. You can't see the stars as well when you move fast down the road.* Vega, Altair, and whatever the third one was, Gamma Globulin, maybe. *They're up there, but you'd never see them by going fast.* Uncle Loyal is better company than I counted on, and again, I think of how much he reminds me of some of the tribal elders, their light touch when shaking hands, how their conversation was filled with long pauses, how they moved little but saw *everything*. Loyal and I survived the storm. Now we have that gauzy sky and a few stars twinkling overhead. I let up on the accelerator again. I wonder what Uncle Loyal had seen that I had missed.

I feel like I am a sea captain, steering a sleek red ship. Stars overhead to guide me through a sea of wheat and corn. The long, low rises in the road are the swells, but there are no waves.

The prairie was an ocean.

It had turned into a beautiful evening for a drive. Why go fast? Why not slow down a little? The six hundred bucks would still be there whether we arrived tomorrow or next week.

Uncle Loyal's mild voice, sandy and sweet, brings me back from my faraway thoughts.

"We'll be with each other for more than a thousand miles, Levi. Tell me something about yourself. I don't know your family very well, a shortcoming all my own. I should have visited more often, stayed better connected. I'd like to become better acquainted with you. Perhaps we'll become fast friends on this journey together, eh?"

"Well . . ." What could I tell him? What *should* I tell him?

Maybe I should tell him just what I am imagining at the moment: Uncle Loyal, you and I are sailors out on an ocean on a small, fast red boat, and I had this very strange idea about driving up to a farmhouse—no, sailing to a harbor, a port—and being welcomed as long-lost friends. Or I could tell him that his fairness, his understanding of silence, and his quiet way remind me of the tribal elders that I had occasion to meet.

Or I could tell him I liked sports, girls, and greasy hamburgers, played too many video games, and that I wear my baseball hat backwards whenever I can.

Junction ahead, Levi. Time for a choice. What do I tell Loyal about me? Would he understand the comparison with the tribal elders? Would he get the whole concept about our fast red schooner sailing across the wheat fields?

I fidget and pretend to concentrate on the road ahead. I still don't quite know how to answer Uncle Loyal. It is so nice, so utterly *cool* to be driving out here in the middle of North Dakota or Detroit or the Yukon or wherever we are. This is like a scene out of Mayberry, me being Opie, Uncle Loyal playing Sheriff Andy, the two of us having a nice little chat on the front porch on a Sunday afternoon with Aunt Bea fussing about a pie.

"Well, I've lived in Utah all my life."

"I thought perhaps so."

"Except for my mission. I went to Arizona, northern part of the state."

"Quite an experience, eh?"

"Yep. I'll graduate next spring with a degree in business."

"Wonderful. I believe I knew that about you also. And after that?"

"Get a job, I suppose. Maybe grad school, but I don't have much money. Money's important when you're just getting started."

"Often a problem, the combination of grad school and finances."

"And I have a friend, a girl-type friend, her name is Rachel, but she's not my *girlfriend*, just a friend who happens to be a female, and when I get back to school, I'd like to see where things go. You know. Like you and Aunt Daisy. Or my parents. See if we get there or not, hook it up, you know, like go to the big dance."

I realized that I had just referred to eternal marriage, creating spirits and worlds without number, making the most important decision of my earthly life and perhaps in my entire existence, as "getting there or not." The feeling of being a philosopher evaporated in a nanosecond. Why could I never quite trust the right words to come tumbling out of my mouth?

"Interesting. I'm sure Rachel is quite taken with someone of your obvious abilities and talents, with your kindness and depth of understanding about life."

"And that's about it. I'm not very interesting or exciting, and this trip with you, I . . ."

I'm doing this for money, Uncle Loyal. That's what I was going to say, but I can't force out the words. *I'm not the person you think I am.* I began to feel awkward. *Really* awkward.

"And?"

"And that's about it for me." I think a few seconds. It was true. That's about all there was to me. Not much to show for twenty-four years of work.

"I see."

My fingers are strumming the steering wheel. I didn't want to tell Uncle Loyal anything more because the conversation might quickly get into areas that would lead him to conclude that I was not a kind person, that my depth of understanding was at the shallow end of the pool. And I was beginning to feel like a creep because I was making this trip with this really nice, old, and wise guy, *and I was doing it just for the money.*

He must have figured out that I had become uncomfortable. He says, "I already feel I know you better. Thank you, Levi." It is a nice little period on the end of a sentence, his way of saying that's fine, that's okay, the conversation, at least this part of it, is over, you don't need to tell me anything more. He puts his hands behind his neck and stretches out. Then he tilts his head back and yawns, and down the long road we go.

We are beyond the edge of civilization. Signs of life disappeared quickly during our short conversation. I couldn't see farmhouses anywhere. It's dark, as dark as it used to get when I was out in the woods on a campout and the last embers of the fire had died down; the only light you saw came from the moon and the stars. The filmy clouds in the sky seems to have disappeared, too. The sky is clear and dazzling. The storm is over.

"In another mile or so, there's a turnout, Levi, a rest area. There are many other stars out tonight. The clouds have vanished. It's always good to view them after a storm. It makes me feel as though the world has been washed; it is fresh, and we have the chance to start all over. It's a funny thought, Levi, certainly odd, I acknowledge. Daisy sometimes told me I imagined too many things, but I always enjoy thinking what perhaps no one else ever has. Let's pull over and take a look up. What do you think? Eh?"

What do I think? Part of me hears the siren call of the six hundred dollars waiting at the end of the road, and the sooner I get there, the faster I have the wad of green clutched in my happy little fists, and Levi becomes one blissful guy. The other part of me wonders why I don't know the name of more stars and why I can't pick out more constellations.

I've had the time to do so. Can't blame it on that. I just haven't done it. Like family history or food storage or waiting until the end of the month to do my home teaching. Human error. Avoidable. But oh so easy.

It will be okay, I think, to drag my feet a little on this trip. I lean forward, bend over the steering wheel, and look at the North Dakota night sky. Even as we bomb down the dark road, I can see what looked like a thousand stars. An image of creation floats into my mind.

Wisdom, at least my brand of it, seems to say, "Pull over and look up at the stars. Uncle Loyal is right. Let's take a look up."

I draw in my breath. I tell my great-uncle something that I can hardly believe, even as I hear my own voice say it.

I tell him, "Yeah, show me where to turn. It's a beautiful night. You're right. We can slow down. Let's go look at the stars."

CHAPTER NINE

WHEN YOU SEE A SHOOTING STAR
YOU MAY BE SEEING YOURSELF

I AM DISCOVERING THIS MUCH: my nephew is a young man capable of surprises. I mentioned the turnout along the highway but didn't expect him to pull in for a chance to look into the night sky. But he agreed. We drove slowly to the darkest part of the rest area and spent a few minutes gazing at the sky. Then, I believe I surprised my grand-nephew by walking to the front of the car, bracing myself, and leaning back until I lay on its hood, my hands folded behind my head to provide a bit of a cushion. Shyly, he came around to the front of the car and did likewise. There we were. Two men on the warm and slightly dirty hood of a car staring straight toward heaven.

I let my eyes adjust to the darkness. I squint, and my eyes dart across the black canvas of the sky overhead. Slowly, it comes to view, begins to make sense, as though we are sorting through the pieces of a vast puzzle. I tell him, "Look there, see that? It's Cygnus, the Swan, and its white giant. And there. Over there. Look there. Do you see it? Sagittarius, the Archer. We have picked a fine night for star gazing," I say.

He looks.

"I can't see an archer. I can't see a swan." Then he looks a little more. We need see no more than a dark summer sky to understand that God works in patterns. Beautiful, precise, and brilliant patterns. Levi begins to put together pieces into a whole. "Oh. Now. Yeah. Maybe I can. I think I see it now. Both of them. I dig this. You connect the dots. Yes, I see."

"Yes. You connect the dots."

The sky had totally cleared; the stars sparkle as though they are jewels scattered on a roll of dark velvet. It is satisfying to introduce my young great-nephew to the stars. I hope he'll remember to look toward heaven on pitch-black nights in future times. I hoped he would learn the beauty of patterns, the strength in slowness, the wonder of pace, the link between wisdom and time.

"We have a long trip ahead. I think we should be getting on our way again," I finally suggest. "Maybe we've seen enough stars for one night."

Levi doesn't move. His head cranes upward, his gaze intent. A half-minute of portentous silence slips by before he finally speaks. "Just another minute, Uncle Loyal." And then, "This is just starting to make sense."

The sense of pace. The peace of slowness. He is beginning to understand lessons that the plains had taught me. I again join him in looking up.

It was then that a silvery white dot of light burst across the sky, moving impossibly fast, producing no sound, making a wild ride across the sky. It seemed to make everything on earth stand still and fall to silence and seem small. We had seen a shooting star, nothing uncommon in North Dakota at that time of the year, but apparently something rarely seen by my great-nephew.

"Wow. Whoa. Wow. Dude, did you see that?"

"I did. Yes."

"I can't ever remember seeing anything like that. That was awesome."

"It was spectacular."

"I've never, never seen one like that. Not at all."

Slowly, he rises from the car hood, our time gazing at stars now capped by an event most memorable. The air smells both sweet and musty. We open the car doors and slide into our places in the front seat.

Levi starts the engine but does not put the car into gear. In the dim light that comes from the dashboard, he turns toward me.

"I wonder what it's like to be a shooting star," he says.

An unusual thought, certainly. But I am happy to hear it. "I think you already know something of it."

He puts the car in gear and presses his foot on the accelerator, and we merge back on to the highway. "Well, we'd better try to make up for lost time. We have a long bit of road ahead of us," he says, and the red car moves down the highway at a faster clip.

"I'm enjoying this. All of it. The trip. The drive. The company." My words come back to him in the humid air, tinged with the peculiar fragrance of dampened corn, near to ripe. I'm not quite sure of the implications, not understanding the idiom of the young, but I enjoy being called "dude" by him. The tone of our trip is changing. It is becoming a journey. And I think this: we have much to learn from each other.

A few more seconds pass before I have the perspicacity to add, "And we have many miles to go."

CHAPTER TEN

AND I WORRIED ABOUT UNCLE LOYAL BEING THE ONE WHO WAS NUTS

I TOLD UNCLE LOYAL, SURE, let's pull onto the driveway and look at the stars. The little voice whined in my mind: *Remember the fat paycheck at the end of the road, Levi. When you waste time, you waste money.* That was Levi the man of business speaking. But Levi the human being fortunately took control. I enjoyed the experience. Give him credit. The old fellow did seem to know tons about the stars. Did you know that Orpheus played the harp really well? The guy must have *rocked*.

So there we were on the side of the road, spread out on the car hood, looking up at the stars, and Uncle Loyal was pointing out some constellations, and I was thinking, *I can't see much, and I've probably had about all I can handle in the way of Dakota culture for one afternoon and evening.* Next thing we'd be stopping at the Cornfields of Mystery, or Wheat fields of Wonder, or some other such roadside attraction, and I'd be buying postcards to send to my friends and let them know what an amazing time I was having.

Then I started to see the patterns, and things began to click for me. So much to see and understand, and I hadn't taken the time to notice. Uncle Loyal had already talked about the slowness of all things, two or three times, and honestly, I thought it was just one of those things nice old guys say. But I now get part of what he means: you *do* see more when you're going slow. Then I saw the star, the shooting star, and for a moment I forgot about where I was, who I was with, what I was doing, what was important to me. I even forgot about the money I was earning on this quick trip. The shooting star was amazing, much more so than any I've seen back home, maybe because the lights are bright there and we never hardly look up.

I have to say it. The shooting star *inspired* me.

And—not to sound too whacked out here—I wondered if I could be my own shooting star in a nice, normal kind of earthly LDS way. *Loyal is getting inside your head, Levi.*

Talk to yourself, Levi. Work through this. Okay. The point is, I'm on track for a lot of things—the mission is over, I'm about to start my last year at school, I have Rachel interested in me and me interested in her, at least I think that's the way it shapes up, and I know I want to be *successful,* but I'm still pulled in different directions. I get pulled in the direction of earning money, having a job with prestige and pizzazz, trophy home, trophy wife, trophy kids, trophy cars, trophy church calling, trophy everything—anything to be above and stand out from others. To be someone. Is that a crime? And then I see that star and think it's what I want to be without being any of it all. It's clear, its course is straight, you can see it but you need to know where to look for it, and when you see it, you admire it, but it does nothing to call attention to itself. It's just there. It's *pure,* and there are no trophies in sight. It's just there. For anyone to look at, if you know *where* to look at the *right* time.

Okay, am I a little nuts here? I worried about Uncle Loyal not having dry mortar between his bricks, but I'm the one who looks at him and says, "See that star? I want to be like it." I want to be a bursting ball of white light in a dark sky. Like a four-year-old who says he wants to be a cowboy or a fireman or a professional basketball player. Me? I want to be a shooting star.

So I sit behind the steering wheel, and I think of what has taken place in the last few hours of my life. I take inventory. I do a little cost accounting. I add things up.

I saw a shooting star and thought I wanted to be like it, which about pegs me off the weirdness meter.

Uncle Loyal fed me a ham sandwich, and it got to me. Who eats a ham sandwich and comes away thinking he's had a significant emotional experience? Me, just me. That's who.

I know what Vega and Altair are, and I think I can find Cygnus on my own. Before tonight, I thought they might be a heavy metal band.

I drove through a crashing storm and saw lightning licking down in cornfields and thunder that sounded like a freight train blasting two inches from my toes.

And I'm not thinking as much about the easy six hundred awaiting me soon after I cross into Davis County and head up the hill to Aunt Barbara's mansion on the ridge.

All of this in a few short hours, with my Uncle Loyal. What if I *do* slow this trip down? How much more would I have to talk about? How many more stars would I see? How many stars and constellations am I missing by going too fast and bracketing my life in dollar signs? How many more stories would I have to tell? How much more would I learn?

And maybe when my friends all started talking about their summers, the jobs they had, their experiences, when they started to shake and bake a little in front of me, I'd just think, *Yeah, but I was with Loyal, and you can't match that, no way man.* Smug.

My career as a boxboy is over. I have latched on to my last mop and cleaned up after little Junior Short Pants for the last time. I have endured my last complaint about the asparagus being crushed by the canned corn or the bananas being too green or the price of lettuce being too high, as if I had any control over it.

Here is the hint, memo to self: Enjoy your time with Uncle Loyal. *The man is a beast.*

I start the car, a thousand thoughts billowing through my mind. Then one thought comes clear, takes hold, and before I know it, I'm asking Uncle Loyal a question that would have been astonishing to me earlier in the day.

"Do you mind if we slow down on this trip? Stretch it out a little? I'm really in no hurry. We've got time."

He gives me that old owl look in the dim light of the car. He scrunches his lips together and gently drums his fingers on his slacks. The gears are turning. I can hear them.

"Not at all, Levi. Not in the slightest. Slow down and gain. That's what I say."

Chapter Eleven
We Decide to Make It a Trip Worth Remembering, Starting with My Friend Glenn

Well. I am surprised. Pleasantly so. Levi seems to be more friendly and thoughtful, or at least thinking more, with every hour we spend together on this long road.

He told me that we'd slow the pace down, take in some sights, be more casual in our travels. He asks me if there was anything I'd particularly like to do.

A good question for a man my age. One must be selective, putting every day to some good use. I certainly have little time to squander. An idea takes form. It has been on my list for many years.

"Something, maybe. Something I've been thinking of for a long time, something I should have done a few years back, when I was younger and more healthy and able to get around better."

"Just tell me. As long as it isn't too far out there, Uncle Loyal."

"I'd like to see my old friend Glenn Leuthold."

"Does he live far out of the way? Not that it matters. We have time, remember? Time. Lots of it. We have it. Time we have, time is us. Am I starting to talk like Yoda?"

"He is a little out of the way. He's in a small town in northeastern Montana."

"Montana? We need to pass through there anyway," Levi says agreeably. "What's a little detour? Your pal Glenn in Montana. It can be done."

"Thank you. Do you have some maps? We can chart our course."

"No maps. Just a little cheap one they gave me when I rented the car, but nothing of Montana. Let's stop. We can stop when we get to the state line; there must be one of those visitor center dealios where they hand out maps. We are now officially tourists."

"You must know something about Glenn . . ."

"Look, man, we're going to get you to Glenn's, no questions, no statements, no buts about it, you will be shaking hands with your pal in no time."

"It's not quite possible to—"

"*Uncle Loyal! Enough!*"

"Okay, but . . . I yield to your indomitable will, Levi. To Glenn's."

"To Glenn's and not another word about it. It's a plan. Will Glenn be at home? I hate to drive a long way and find out your friend isn't there. That would be a major disappointment."

"Oh, he'll be there. I'm not worried. Glenn doesn't get around much."

Glenn and I became acquaintances, then friends, many decades ago, somewhere around junior high school years. I first remember him from Mrs. Jansen's English class. To this day, I still quiver when I think of Mrs. Jansen, the perfect caricature of a schoolmarm. Tall, stern, bosomy, thin glasses, hair in a bun, pinned the same way each day. She had five dresses that she wore to school, one for each day of the week. I still recall them—plain, coarse woolen garments, one gray, one black, one blue, one a darker gray, and the last a darker blue. You could look at her dress and know exactly which day of the week it was: Dark gray? It is Thursday.

She was a large woman, starch fed, a commanding presence, queen of her domain, and we students, her peasants, to do with as she pleased. She suffered no fools, and fools we all were. I can still hear the clop, clop, clop of her sturdy, sensible, black shoes pacing the aisles between our desks, her hawk eyes missing nothing. Her tongue was sharp, her wrath unbearable. Those who endured her class forged a bond and a closeness that only comes with survival of harsh elements, those who experienced something akin to death yet lived to tell about it.

Although credit her with this: we could parse sentences in our sleep, repeat precisely the definition of a gerund, participle, and adverbial clause, and would rather suffer a slow, tortuous passing than split an infinitive in her presence.

I was chief among her fools, although all of us felt her righteous indignation. We were fodder for Mrs. Jansen's grammarian blasts. Of all her pupils, though, Glenn had the greatest knack for grammar. Though far from being the teacher's pet—Mrs. Jansen had none, her wickedness allowed no favorites, her heart no tender mercies—he emerged from her class the least bruised and bloodied.

Mrs. Jansen's most terrifying teaching ploy was to call out five names, bark out five sentences, and send the quavering students to the chalkboard to diagram a sentence. On a grim, fall Dakota morning, my name was among the unfortunates. To this day, more than sixty-five years later, I recall the sentence she assigned me: The pilot flew his plane high above the cornfields but beneath the layer of clouds.

I trudged to the board, unsure of where to begin, other than recognizing the starting point: *pilot*, the noun. In a rare lapse of concentration, Mrs. Jansen trudged back to her desk and was distracted by a pile of papers lying on it. Face to the blackboard, chalk in trembling hands, I wrote *pilot*. I turned slightly. From the corner of my eye, I saw Glenn mouth the words "flew his plane" and nod slightly toward where the phrase needed to be placed. A couple more deft hand signals and a tiny jerk of his head, and my sentence was on the board, completed.

And completed correctly.

"I am surprised, Mr. Wing. But in a good way. Our hard work seems to be paying off," Mrs. Jansen said moments later when reviewing my effort. It was the closest brush to praise her dark soul would allow. "You may have more than thistledown between the ears. Surprised. Yes, I am." I stammered a thank-you and took my place behind my wood-and-iron school desk.

At that moment, I knew I had a friend in Glenn Leuthold.

Through the years, we gathered together many more memories, and our friendship took on a depth to match a swelling ocean. We became friends, then buddies. Glenn was the skinny, smooth-shooting forward on our raggedy high school basketball team; I was one of the starting guards. We rode our horses to school together until our junior years, his a buckskin, mine a little gray. We double-dated the Hecht sisters, Judy and Lois, to the prom our senior year, ending up at the Leutholds' house in the late hours of the night, laughing, playing board games, drinking root beer floats, and feeling, perhaps for the first time, a bit like adults in those simpler, cleaner times.

The summer after our graduation, only weeks after our prom dates with the Hecht sisters, with a dark cloud over Europe and the black froth in the South Pacific, we enlisted in the navy, with high hopes for training together and ending up stationed together. It was not meant to be: I spent most of my tour on a minesweeper, while Glenn ended up on an Aleutian Island, as far away from the warm Pacific waters and tropical temperatures as he could get. The Hecht sisters, for whom our fancies flew, married while we were away, to light-headed local boys judged by the draft board unfit for war. We mourned separately, and we mourned together in our letters. If only they had waited. We offered prospects that the local war-less boys could not match.

After the war, we both went to school. Pharmacy for me, agriculture for Glenn. He used his little savings to buy a small farm in eastern Montana, while I settled in as the town druggist in the upper right-hand corner of North Dakota. But we never seemed far from one another, as is the case with true friends.

Yes, it would be good to again be in Glenn Leuthold's presence. We survived a war together; we survived Mrs. Jansen's English class together. The war was the tougher of the two, no doubt, but the gap between these two milestones in our lives is probably not as wide as one might first think.

Glenn's friendship was patient, enduring, forgiving, and marked by sacrifice. There were times to be talked over with him once more. In my new Utah home, there will be few chances to visit him.

"Uncle Loyal?"

Levi interrupts my reverie about days gone by, older times, older ways.

"A map. Remember? When we get to the state line, we'll need a map of Montana. I should've got a GPS for the car."

"I think I can find my way there. Daisy and I visited Glenn and his wife often, until the last few years. It's an interesting drive."

"Whatever. I'd still like a map, though. This is all new country to me. One wrong turn and we could end up in Saskatchewan. I think that's a place. In Canada. Two wrong turns, and we could end up in Nova Scotia, which is also a place. In Canada."

"We'll keep our eyes open for a rest area where we can get a map."

We continue down the two-lane highway. It's edging toward midnight. Levi's face looks drawn in the glow of the dashboard lights. I feel sleepy but try to stay awake to keep him company. He had taken a nap, but this is a time of the night when even my young nephew is accustomed to sleeping.

We drive another twenty miles, rumbling past farms and fields, splitting the wide night in two with our headlights. Levi yawns once, then a second time. His head bobs up and down. He blinks hard. He shakes his head and yawns a third time. Ahead of us, off to the side of the highway, I see the bright lights of a truck stop tucked into a corner where our road intersects with another. As we near, I see a sign flashing, "Open 24 hours." Behind the pumps and the restaurant, I see a small motel.

"I think it's time that we get some rest, Levi. I'm feeling the effects of a long day. There's a motel ahead, just beyond the truck stop. A few hours there and we'll both feel like young pups. I'm sure you're up to the drive, but I am most definitely sleepy. What do you think? Eh?"

He nods. He puts up no resistance. Without a word, he flips on his turn signal, and we hear the crunch of the pebbled parking lot underneath our tires. My window is down slightly, and the air smells of grease, oil, gasoline, and heavy food. Rumbling diesel engines idle. Bright light spills over our red car. I hear the deep voice of a man shouting across the din. And yet the garish lights and smell of fuel beckon to the weary travelers.

I sigh and think of the irony.

My first home away from home will be a truck stop.

CHAPTER TWELVE

I AM INSPIRED BY AMAZING HELMET HAIR, THE LIKES OF WHICH I HAVE NEVER SEEN BEFORE

UNCLE LOYAL WAS RUNNING OUT of steam, poor guy. I should have expected it. I peeked at him a few times, and his head was nodding and his eyes were closed. Sleepy time, sweet man. Me? I was fine. My nap gave me that second wind, and I felt like I could have driven all night long, down the dark highway, straight as a kite string, until we ended up in Podunk, Montana—or whatever it's called—and I deposited Uncle Loyal on the doorstep of his friend Glenn.

I could tell that Uncle Loyal was tight with this fellow Glenn. He talked a little bit about them, what they did in school together, how they doubled to the prom (Prom? Did they have proms in North Dakota? In the 1930s? Must have. Loyal wouldn't lie. Maybe they rode there on the back of a dinosaur.), and how they joined the Navy together, a couple of kids from the plains, neither of whom had even so much as seen the ocean, and then, there they were, floating on top of it.

And I liked the thought of Loyal and Glenn getting together, the handshake, the hug, the how-are-yous, you-look-greats, how-about-that-corn-crop-this-year. I could dig it. These two old guys, seeing each other for maybe the last time. I'd just sit back quietly and watch it happen, drink it in. If it meant staying the whole day and maybe even a night in Podunk, I was cool with it. Time. Remember, I am not counting time on this trip. The check will be there tomorrow for me, and it will be there next week. Doesn't matter. Does it?

Slow down and gain. Isn't that what Uncle Loyal told me?

We pull into the motel parking lot, which was covered in rock. The blazing, blinking red light over the office is missing a letter, so the sign reads, "Of ice." Loyal and I get out of our car and wander into the "Of ice." I fish out the credit card Aunt Barbara had given me from of my jeans' pocket, a little bent but still plenty useful. The heavy hum of several big diesel engines fills the smelly, oily air.

We walk into the office, and there sits a woman, fiftyish, with blue cat-eye glasses and the largest beehive hairdo that has ever existed in, and I am certain of this, the entire history of the universe. It was lacquered in place with what must have been two cans of hair spray, every strand in its perfect position. Mechanical engineers could have had a field day just by studying her blue top. A Little League baseball team could have hidden in it. It might have been a silo for missiles. It should have been, at the very least, designated a national historical monument. She chews gum as she scans the lines of a paperback romance novel. I know her name. I absolutely know it.

I know her name is Evelyn. It had to be. Some things are just decreed by the universe, and this was one of them. Evelyn.

I stand there in dumb admiration and awe of her amazing hair. After we approached the desk, she looked up at the two of us. Her name tag said, "Welcome, I am Evelyn." I feel at one with the universe. I check the calendar, which has a painting of a man in a plaid hunting jacket next to his retriever. The dog has big brown eyes, tail up, and a dead pheasant in its mouth. I check the calendar to make sure it doesn't say 1956.

I half expect a slim, serious man to step out from the side somewhere and say, "Two men, traveling across the Dakotas. Little did they know they had traveled much farther than they thought, on a road that possibly had no end. Back through time. Back through the ages. Back into the Twilight Zone . . ."

Uncle Loyal just stands there pleasantly smiling, not realizing, or at least not showing it, that he is in the presence of greatness in the form of Evelyn's two-story-tall pile of blue lacquered hair. I fight the urge to fall down on my knees and worship her.

"Well?" she says, between chomps on her gum, glancing up from the bodice-ripping romance novel.

"A room. Do you have a room for us, a couple of twin beds?" Uncle Loyal asks politely. "We've driven a long way. We've had quite the day, and a little rest would do the two of us good. Nonsmoking, please."

"Lemme check."

She turns, looks at a Peg-Board behind her, and reaches for a key. "Room ten is available. Queen bed and a sleeper couch. Thirty-six dollars, plus tax. Interested?"

For a moment, neither of us answers. I can't keep my eyes off her hair, her glasses, her orange nail polish, the bad makeup. Loyal clears his throat and tosses me a quick glance. I realize that he can't answer because I have Aunt Barbara's credit card. With what I'd like to think was great inner strength, I take my eyes off her blue honeycombed hair and say, "That'll be fine." I resist the urge to ask her how long it took her to fix up her hair, how many crates of hair spray she owns, and if she is busy after she gets off work.

I have to admit it. Evelyn intrigued me. I have never met anyone like her. Or at least anyone with that kind of hair.

She hands me the key, I scribble my name on the credit card slip, and after one long, respectful glance back at the Mount Everest of hair, Uncle Loyal and I are back in the car, reaching for our suitcases. We straggle into the room, which was everything you'd expect for a thirty-six-buck special after midnight in North Dakota—brown wood panels; the faint odor of smoke; a faded, bad painting on the wall of a lonesome calf looking for its mother; plaid, greasy sheets; and a window air conditioner that has a rattle loud enough to be heard across three states.

"It's not a five-star, Uncle Loyal."

"No, but it will do. A few hours of rest and we'll be good to go."

"Did you notice . . . the woman, and . . . her hair?"

"It would have been hard not to. It was rather impressive. My, but that hair was intriguing."

"Rather impressive? You're killing me, Uncle Loyal. It should be on the cover of *National Geographic*. A small country might be housed in there. I bet it could stand a nuclear bomb hit. I've never seen anything like it." I pause. I decide to have a bit of fun with Uncle Loyal. I think of just how to say what I'm going to say next, the right words, the right feeling to express myself completely and eloquently. "It's like this. Uncle Loyal, I think I'd like to date her."

He tilts his head back and laughs softly. "I think you need someone more your own age. Your infatuation for her will pass, despite that magnificent hair. I'm certain of that."

"I'd like to have the hair spray franchise for around here."

"You'd make a good bit of money on just one customer."

"Wonder why she fixes it up that way."

"Her hair is very important to her. She must put in much time and effort to maintain it in the manner she does."

"Could it be a wig?"

"Eh. No, it was hers. I've seen too many wigs in my years in the pharmacy. Cancer patients, chemotherapy. I can tell a wig, even a good one, from a ways off. Miss Evelyn does not wear a wig. I can tell. Her hair is her own. All of it, Levi, in its full glory."

"I bet you *can* tell real hair from fake hair. You noticed her name. You find her attractive, Uncle Loyal. Admit it."

"Attractive, yes. I believe all people are, often in different ways. What I see is a woman who is expressive. Her hair gives her expression. I am quite sure she is a most interesting young woman."

"Expression or attention?"

"Expression. I believe it's all about expression. We all need it in some way. For our friend the motel clerk, it comes in the form of that wonderful hair. I am sure she checks it often, takes great care in the way she fixes it. I think her hair is marvelous."

I hadn't quite thought of the clerk's hair in terms of "marvelous," but I guess it was. Expression, Uncle Loyal says. I decide to play along with him a little more. I had to admit it; I am having *fun* clowning around with Uncle Loyal. Who would have guessed?

"I'm feeling as though something magical happened in the office tonight, Uncle Loyal."

"In what way?"

"It was destiny that I met Evelyn, the motel clerk."

"That is wonderful, Levi. Few things in life are pure coincidence. Perhaps you can express your thoughts to her when we check out in the morning. I imagine she has many admirers, particularly among those who drive trucks for a living."

"It's going to be a long night. Thinking of Evelyn and her hair, all piled up like that."

"It will make for pleasant dreams, although you said you're not tired. As for me, I'd like to turn in. I thought ahead enough to pack some pajamas. If you'll excuse me, I'll go into the bathroom and change into them. I'm ready for a snooze."

"Go ahead. I may just skip the formalities and head straight for the sleeper. Maybe I am a little zonked. Toss some *Z*s up in the air before you can blink your eyes."

Uncle Loyal changes his clothing and comes back toward the bed. He is wearing some plaid cotton pajamas and slippers. He gingerly sits on the edge of the bed.

"The bed or the sleeper sofa. I'll flip a coin with you," he says.

"Okay."

I take a quarter out of my pocket and flip it straight up in the air. Uncle Loyal calls out "Tails."

I catch the coin and open my hand slowly. It was heads. "I lose, you win. You get the bed. I'll curl up on the sleeper."

"I must point out a technicality. I didn't see the coin, Levi."

"You accuse me of lyin', stranger? Them's fighting words in these here parts, wherever we are in these here parts."

"Not lying. Just not telling the truth. There is a subtle but important difference."

"Prove it. And smile when you say that, pardner. We don't take to people not smilin' when they're callin' a man a liar. In these parts. Wherever these parts are."

"I can't prove it." Then he gives me a big, cheesy grin.

"Sue me."

"I won't. You have no money. And I don't want any anyway."

"Let's arm wrestle for the bed."

"I shouldn't."

"Coward."

"Smile when you say that, my young, rambunctious friend."

I walk over to him. We square our arms on the little nightstand and lock fingers.

"One, two . . ."

And before "three" is pronounced, I flip my arm backwards, in the direction *his* arm needed to go in order to win. Uncle Loyal is not fooled.

"You cheated. Not a fair match. Not very manly of you, Levi. And I shall not smile when I say that. You are a cheat and a liar."

"I know. But I'm not very manly."

"I demand a rematch."

"You're not going to get it. You're licked. Face it. Our town was a nice little place in wherever we are until you rode in. Then things changed. It just ain't no good here now. It don't feel right no more. I'll be fine on the sleeper."

"So would I. I insist."

"I had a nap, which you didn't. Uncle Loyal, it is your bedtime. Go to bed. Don't argue with me, or I'll ground you."

Good grief. I opened my mouth, and my father came out. Uncle Loyal gives me a slow, wise grin.

"I know when I'm beat, Levi. Or 'licked,' as you would say. Whippersnapper."

"It takes a mighty big man to admit when he's licked."

"You only won because you cheated. And because you were untruthful."

"I know. I couldn't beat you fair and square so I cheated. Deal with it, Uncle Loyal. Get over it. It's a mean and cruel world. Dog eat dog. You're old enough to know that."

"Good night, Levi."

"Good night, Uncle Loyal."

I fall onto the sleeper sofa, and it's a bit like doing a belly flop into a swimming pool, the kind of dive that leaves you with red marks on your stomach, gasping for air. The springs probably qualify as antiques. The mattress has more lumps in it than day-old cream of wheat.

"Mmm. Feels good. I'll be asleep in no time." I force a dreamy mumble and fake a yawn. I was enjoying my newly found talent of not quite telling the truth.

Uncle Loyal switches off the lamp and crawls under the blankets. The air conditioner rattles, the diesel truck engines rumble, and somewhere, maybe from the twenty-four-hour café adjacent to the office, some bad country music is playing. Some sappy guy singing about his ex-girl, his ex–dog, his ex–best friend who stole them both and drove off in his ex–pickup truck, and how he saw the flag and it made him weep, then he heard his ex-dog yelp, all wrapped up into one bad song. Somehow, it all fit.

Then I had trouble remembering anything. A fatigue comes over me as though I had been up all night, which, come to think of it, I pretty much had. Bed springs that were made at the time Lewis and Clark strolled through this neighborhood don't matter. Nor does the clackety air conditioner. I close my eyes, and in the ether of diesel fumes, deep-fried food, who knows what other assorted toxins, and whatever was spewing from the air conditioner, my head drops. Let's see . . . somewhere in North Dakota, the motel, the red car, the tornado. I struggle to grasp just where I am. And one more thing . . . oh yes. Evelyn, the empress of big hair. Now, I grew up in Utah, a place where big hair is understood, respected, and adored. I have some experience in this matter. I close my eyes once again and have a vision: a two-foot-high stack of bluish beehive-bun hair on Evelyn's head.

Yes, I think dreamily, Uncle Loyal was right. It was marvelous.

When I awake, it is a few minutes past six in the morning.

CHAPTER THIRTEEN

I TELL LEVI WHAT I KNOW ABOUT LOVE

LEVI WAS SHOWING SURPRISING CHARACTER. He rightfully could have taken the softer bed, but he wouldn't. We had quite the conversation about who would sleep where. In the end, I accused him of cheating on a coin flip, something that he gleefully acknowledged. And then, with insouciance, he ignored me and hopped onto the sleeper sofa after purposefully throwing an arm wrestling contest. I could hear the ancient springs underneath the sofa bed creak and groan. I'm sure it was uncomfortable, and I worried that he would get no rest. We needed him to be fresh. We had too many miles to go for the driver to feel tired.

I slept well for a few hours, but it was a noisy motel. About six in the morning, it seemed that every driver in the parking lot began to rev his engine. Business at the small restaurant, only a dozen yards or so away from our room, picked up. The talk was loud, friendly, knowing, and profane. Still, it seemed that Levi was asleep, so I lay quietly, my eyes on the ceiling, watching the first gray light of a late summer day filter into the room. I think of my home and how I miss it. I think of Daisy and wonder if she is near, if she can see what is going on, and if she is laughing softly at the sight of me in a truck stop. I wonder again if I have made a mistake by leaving my home. And part of me, I confess, wonders if God in His starry heaven knew my travails and heard my prayers.

I knew the answers to those questions, but nonetheless, I find myself asking Him. He sends little guidance, which is what I expected. I am left only with the thought, "Struggle through this as well, Loyal. You've been through more difficult. I will require not an ounce more than what you need to endure. Struggle through."

And so I vow again, for what must have been the thousandth time, to struggle through. This enduring. It is not easy. It is not comfortable. Yet it must be.

The springs on the sofa sleeper groan as Levi turns. I hear him sniff, see movement from the corner of my eye. I know he's awake, ready to face the day with verve and vigor.

"Uncle Loyal?" he whispers.

"Eh, Levi?"

"You must be awake."

"I am. I have been for a while. I didn't want to disturb you."

"I've been awake for a while too. Can't stop thinking. Stop thinking at all. She is magnificent. I want to see her again."

"Who? The young lady you mentioned yesterday? Rachel, I think you called her."

"No, not Rachel."

I sit up in bed. He turns over and looks at me. Mirth is in his drowsy, downy eyes. He rubs his unshaven jaw thoughtfully. "Her."

"Who?"

"Who? She who. That's who. Evelyn."

"The desk clerk last night? She of the wondrous hairstyle?"

"Yep. She's the one. All that hair, built up with as much care as the pyramids and maybe with the approximate same number of workers. I'm thinking we need to date."

"You don't say."

"I do say. My world is rocked. My world is spinning."

"Love. This thing called love. How do you know?"

He flops over on his back and gazes at the ceiling. I acknowledge that I am enjoying this conversation.

"It's her hair. It's something a man could be proud of. Walking into a movie or a restaurant or even church. People would stop and gawk and talk. It's Evelyn's hair. No one could ever sit behind her at a movie. We could house orphans from Asia in it. They could have their own rooms. She might have a fast-food restaurant hidden up there. Fries to go."

I play along with him. I know Levi is only teasing me, but I am beginning to understand his slightly unhinged sense of humor. "She's much older than you."

"What does age matter when it's true love? Evelyn and Levi. We both have the *v* thing going in our first name. How much more of a sign can you have than that?"

"Definitely a sign, Levi. Take it a step further. There's a *v* in *love*."

"You're a genius. Absolutely. I knew you'd see it my way, Uncle Loyal. You were there when we met. We'll name our first child Loyal. I hope it's a boy. I hope he inherits his mother's hair. Little Loyal. He'll be a cute little tyke. With amazing hair. Piles of it."

"No doubt."

He sits up in bed, broad smile, eyes alive. He is chatty. There are no walls, no suspicions. He views us as equals, I believe, for the first time on this trip.

"How do you know you're in love, Uncle Loyal?"

I think about this one for a few moments. Love is not always an easy thing to speak of.

I know his question has nothing to do with Evelyn and everything to do with the young lady Rachel. So I think with care. I think about Daisy and my girls and my friend Glenn. I think of others, too, but mostly Daisy. And I come to a single thought, which came from a feeling, which, as near as I can tell, is how God talks to us most of the time.

"My answer might not make much sense. Or it might not be the sort of dramatic revelation you're looking for. It doesn't have much to do with big hair."

"How did you fall in love with Aunt Daisy? How did you know?"

"Now there's a story."

"Tell me."

I turn toward him. I pull down the long sleeves of my pajamas. I clear my throat. And then I say, "I fell in love with Daisy because I had to."

"Had to? You're wuffin' me, Uncle Loyal. Had to? No way."

"It's true. I am not wuffin' you, although I am unsure what that means. It goes like this."

And then I tell him. I tell him after the war, after a mission, after most of school was done, I heard of a young woman named Daisy who lived in a town about eighty miles away. I heard she was single, pretty, and most of all, an active Church member. I told him my choices and chances were limited in those days, so I got in my car one morning at six and drove the eighty miles to be at her small ward in time for Sunday School.

"You drove eighty miles to see her? You didn't have any more intel than that?"

"Yes. And no. That's all I knew of her. I wasn't even sure of her last name."

"What happened when you got there?"

So I tell Levi some more. I tell him I arrived and sat down in the small chapel, across from where I assumed most people would walk in. I wanted an unobstructed view. I watched people straggle in for twenty minutes. Big farmers in tight, cheap suits. Their wives in cotton floral-pattern dresses. Little children, somber and tired. A young couple, very young, holding hands and cooing to one another.

But no Daisy. Or at least no one who looked anything close to a single young woman with light red hair, as she had been described to me.

"Who told you about her?"

"Our high counselor. His name was Brother Wells. Leland Wells. He pulled me aside after church one day and said, 'There's someone you need to meet. She lives a fair piece from here, but you need to meet her. You need to get up early and make the drive and meet her because you should. That's all I have to say to you on the subject. I believe I am inspired in my advice. Go next Sunday.'"

"So your high councilman set you up on a blind date? That's cool. I always wondered if those guys did anything good."

"Brother Wells was as fine a man as I have known."

"Tell me more. You're at church, staring at the door, waiting for your EP to walk in, but so far, nothing."

"EP?"

"Eternal partner."

"Oh. I see. Young LDS lingo."

"Yeah. But back to the story."

So I tell him more.

I tell him this: The opening hymn was playing. I picked up the hymnal. To this day, I remember what song we sang: 'You Can Make the Pathway Bright,' hymn number 228. A stout, middle-aged man offered the opening prayer, obviously a man of the land, judging by his tanned, wrinkled skin and thick, strong hands. His name was Schallenkamp, a fine German name. I remember that, too, after all these years. I was thinking, "I drove all this way to meet her, to see her, because she is perhaps the only young woman within a hundred mile radius that I could possibly wed. And now she is not here, and I am feeling foolish." But I should have shown more faith because the Lord often allows us to feel foolish just before He blesses and enlightens us.

The man who prayed said, "And may the righteous desires of our hearts be granted," and then he said amen, and then I opened my eyes, and then I heard a rustling and noticed movement near the door at the back of the chapel.

And I turned and I saw her.

"And I loved her at that moment, from then on, from then on until forever."

"That soon? Love at first sight? That doesn't sound like you, Uncle Loyal."

"It was a bit out of character for me. I am not a rash man, and I prefer slowness to haste."

"Then what?"

So I go on with my story. I tell my grandnephew this: It wasn't the *way* she looked, it was *how* she looked. She had on a white dress with a blue sash. She was wearing high heels and wobbling a bit on them. Her eyes, the word I'd describe them with is *serene*. She seemed to be looking for someone in the congregation. It wasn't obvious, just the way her head moved slightly from one side to the other, scanning the room. When her gaze came toward me, her eyes seemed to settle for the slightest pause. I could feel my heart thumping and wondered if I were all right. Then, she and her mother and father took seats on the back row. It was hard for me to see her then, without being too obvious.

The thought came to me that Leland Wells had talked with her, spoken with her parents, mentioned that I might be coming to church that day, that he had prepared the way for me. The thought came to me that she had purchased or sewn a new dress, was wearing high-heeled shoes for possibly the first time in her life. The thought came to me that she couldn't be more than nineteen or twenty years old. The thought came to me that she also understood that something great and cosmic and eternal might occur that day, and she was excited and spellbound and curious about the thought and possibilities. On the plains, in those days, there weren't many opportunities, I told Levi. You had to be prepared for the few that came along.

"That's a great story, Uncle Loyal. She must have looked amazing."

"It wasn't what she looked like, Levi. She was pretty, but it is how the moment felt to me that I still recall."

"Felt?"

"Yes, felt."

"How so?"

So I explain further.

I say to him that I felt sweetness and peace, and my thoughts were clear. I felt excitement, true, but it was also a sense of deep satisfaction.

"That sounds a little weird."

"But it's not. You must understand sweetness in life. Much of my life has been devoted to finding sweetness. To maintain it. To fend off circumstances that would take it from me."

"I'm not sure I follow."

"I wouldn't expect you to. But you will understand. Someday."

"Sweetness."

"Yes."

"And what else, since we're talking about all this? Any more advice?"

"When she walked into the room, it lit up. And she continued to light my life for the rest of hers. It came to this: I chose her and she chose me, and then we worked hard to make it all come together. Now do you see that we *had* to get married? We were each other's only prospect. And it was meant to be."

"Yep. I see. Quite the pair. She lit you up. Like Evelyn lit up my life."

"But only because of her hair. That doesn't count. You must push your horizons further, Levi. You cannot fall in love based on the considerable size of a woman's hair, splendid though it may be."

"Are you saying it's not going to work out with Evelyn?"

"I confess to having some doubts about your future with the lovely Evelyn. Grave doubts, to be completely truthful."

"I suppose not. I hope she doesn't take our breakup too hard. I'll have to leave her a note. 'Evelyn, this is Levi, and despite the *v* our names share, and despite everything that we have between us, and all that we felt about each other, I need to move along in life and drive my Uncle Loyal to see his buddy Glenn today. I'll remember you always, and especially I'll remember your hair always, and if you ever decide to rent a room in it, let me know. Do you have air conditioning up there?' Then I'd sign it, 'Everlastingly yours, Levi, the guy who checked in at midnight with the old fellow.' No offense, Uncle Loyal."

"None taken. I *am* an old fellow. It is fine to call a thing what that thing is."

"What could have been. It was a beautiful experience. In time, she'll get over me and move on with her life. But it won't be easy for either of us."

"Nor would I expect it to be."

"So we'd better get rolling. We've got almost three hundred miles to Glenn's."

"Yes. A good day of driving and visiting ahead of us. But one thing, if I might ask. Your friend Rachel."

Levi swings his feet over the sleeper bed and they thud on the floor.

"Rachel. It's like this, I need to find out. I'm unsure. I don't know," he said.

"If you need to ask, then you understand what the answer probably is."

"I don't know her well enough."

"You'll know when you know."

"Huh?"

"Does the room light up?"

"I think so. I'm not sure, though."

"Is there a sweetness to life when you are around her?"

"Same deal. Not sure. Maybe. Possibly. Could be."

"Then you need to find out. You need to see her in all four seasons."

"Okay, okay. I need to find out. I made her a promise when I left for home."

"I don't need to know the promise. But I hope you are sincere about it."

Levi looks me square in the face. I may have offended him by my choice of words. I certainly didn't mean to. But I saw another side of him. A good side. One not so flippant, not so casual, one that was more mature.

"I don't make promises lightly," he says. "I mean what I say."

Our time for talk is over. We had covered much ground. From Evelyn to Daisy to Rachel, from one corner of love to another. But it's clear he wants this particular topic to be brought to a conclusion. I oblige him. He has enough to think about now.

"I suppose we can get some good greasy food in the restaurant next door. Are you up for a quart of grease and your monthly supply of fat and cholesterol?"

"Let's go. I am starving."

Levi flops onto his knees and says his prayers.

I follow his example.

Then we get cleaned up and eat at the truck stop café, where the food was indeed heavy, filling, and tasty. My sandwich from the night before had long ago worn off.

By eight in the morning, with the sun a dazzling yellow-white and the promise of what might be ahead of us, we are packing the fast red car.

A cheerful, middle-aged man wearing a ball cap that advertised a crop pesticide checks us out of the motel.

"You boys have a good drive today, and come back, see us, next time you're in these parts," he says encouragingly.

Levi lets out a long, exaggerated sigh as we turn back onto the state highway. Two blue lanes and yellow broken stripes ahead of us point toward the Montana line.

Evelyn, I imagine, is asleep somewhere, locked far away in her dreams, her hair long and limp and lying spread upon her pillow, blissfully unaware that Levi and I are leaving her life.

CHAPTER FOURTEEN

NOW I KNOW WHY
GLENN LEUTHOLD WILL BE AT HOME

WE GOT OFF A LITTLE before nine. The sun felt hot, even in the early morning. The two lanes of blacktop were oily and shimmery in the distance. We pass by little lakes, really nothing more than ponds, with incredible amounts of wild birds. Uncle Loyal calls the tiny lakes "potholes," and they pockmark the prairie every few hundred yards. We rumble through the tiny North Dakota towns—Starkweather, Cando, Maza, and more—before turning west on Highway 2 and blasting toward Minot. The red car zips along the road. Uncle Loyal rolls down his window, and it is fun to see, from the corner of my eye, what was left of his wispy hair whipping around in the wind. We see sad little homes and boarded-up businesses in almost every town we pass through. It makes me feel empty and aching inside to know that people with dreams once lived and worked in them, and now the dreams were gone and maybe the people too.

Uncle Loyal, though, seems happier than the day before. I get the feeling he was down on the first part of our drive, and I can't blame him, leaving his home, his town, his friends, and heading off to Utah. I have to admit, I wonder how he will do in Utah, how he'll fit in. There must be a hundred thousand old guys just like him. Nothing special, most people would think of him. But I know better. I know he is special. Maybe they *all* are special.

I wonder, too, if Aunt Barbara was moving him to Utah for his benefit or to somehow feel more at ease with her own self. You think of people and why they do the things they do. Sometimes you like the answer, and sometimes you don't.

I'm beginning to sound like Uncle Loyal.

Darn. I'm starting to understand this problem I have. *I didn't want to care for him. I didn't want to get involved.* You know my theme: The Easiest Six Hundred Dollars Ever. And now I'm worried about him, hoping that

Utah will work for him, that he'll have some friends to hang out with, stuff to do. I understood how much I was trying to fool myself, how much I didn't want to connect with him, but I *like* the old fellow. I'm not sure I like what I see ahead for him.

This will not be an easy six hundred dollars. Scratch my original theme and start over.

We had a good talk that morning. He told me a lot about life. He told me, in so many words, what I needed to see in Rachel, and she in me, if things were to work out for us.

What did he say?

The room would light up for me whenever she walked in.

That I would know I knew.

That if I had to ask, something wasn't right.

Something about sweetness, sweetness in life, seeing her in four seasons, and making our decision right.

I imagine Rachel, and if she would prefer the man who picked up Loyal and wanted to drive straight through to Utah and cash in or the man who is driving about two hundred miles out of his way so Loyal can see his old pal Glenn. And it tells me something about me, as well. I wanted her to prefer the guy who could deliver Loyal to Glenn.

Uncle Loyal said something that got to me. Something about taking promises lightly. I must have shown I didn't care for what he said because I saw his hand roll into a fist and his jaw tighten slightly. I also knew he felt bad because he quickly changed the topic of our conversation.

I may be a flake at times, but I remember telling him that I don't make light promises. I think he believed me. My word is good, I think, and I hope.

We cruise down the state highway. Uncle Loyal pulls a map out of his deep, baggy pocket and waves it in the air. "Voila!" he says. "A map of the Big Sky country. Seek, and ye shall find."

"Where did you get it? Awesome."

"In a rack as we checked out. When you were paying the bill, I spied it in the corner. It was free. We now know where we're going. To Glenn's."

"To Glenn's!" I shout over the sound of wind whooshing through the open window, and I raise my hand in the air and he smacks it in a perfect high five. "Pedal to the metal, we'll be in Minot for lunch, easy. Then we'll zip right into Montana on Highway 2, and we'll have you at Glenn's in time for a walk around the block, the exchange of grandbaby photos, a tall, cool lemonade, and out for supper," I cheerfully call to Uncle Loyal above the whipped-wind frenzy. "And I'll buy," I add, smug in the knowledge of the yellow credit card in my pocket.

"Very generous of you, Levi. My thanks," Uncle Loyal said. "Glenn doesn't have much of an appetite these days. I doubt he'll be hungry. I really should tell you something more of him. The truth of the matter is that Glenn is . . ."

"*Forget about it!* I told you I'd get you there. I keep my promises, remember? Now just where is it that Glenn lives?"

"A little beyond the town of Glasgow. Maybe a hundred miles past the Montana border. A little wide spot in the road. That's where we'll find him."

My mood and feelings soar. I want to meet Glenn, listen to him talk with Uncle Loyal, swap stories, tell each other how great they looked, recount their war stories and their double dates with the amazing Hecht sisters. For the briefest of moments, I wonder about Glenn, what he will be like. Probably a lot like Loyal. And that was good.

The sun rises higher in the August sky. First it was warm outside; then it turned hot. I switch on the air conditioning. Uncle Loyal looks content as we zoom down the North Dakota blacktop, moving ever closer to Montana. I dream of what Montana must look like—mountains, of course, snow still at the tops of their peaks that were shaking and dancing in the heat against the bright blue sky. Lakes and rivers filled with fish, steep roads that crawled up the sides of black jagged mountains. Cool air, fresh with pine. It is too good a vision to keep to myself.

"Have you ever spent much time in Montana?"

Uncle Loyal looks over at me. "Very little. Mostly I've passed through. I never really stopped to see the sights."

"We've got the time. We should take a look around the place. We're in no hurry, remember? All the time in the world."

"Yes. All the time in the world."

"Big mountains, big fish. Have you ever been fishing, Uncle Loyal?"

"Some. Not much, Levi. A little fishing for bass and sunfish in ponds. Nothing more than that."

"Whoa! Are you kidding me? You've never been creek fishing? Never snagged a rainbow trout? Never stood in water that reaches up to your hips, knocks you off balance, and jerked in a fat fish? Never?"

"Never, Levi."

"Never?"

"Never."

"Then it's time you did. You have missed one of life's biggies."

I could hardly believe what I was thinking, and before I knew it, the words came tumbling out of my mouth.

"Well, we're headed to Montana, and there is no way you and I are going to leave that state without standing in a cold stream catching some fish. Trout fish. No mamby-pamby sunfish from a Dakota pond."

"We have no gear, Levi. And I know you are in a hurry to get home."

"Gear, schmear, who cares. We'll buy some. Utah has fish too. We'll get you to Utah and head up Provo Canyon or hike in the High Uintas. It's time you learned how to fish, Loyal Wing. An important part of your education is lacking. You are among the unwashed, the uncouth, the uncultured. You are a Luddite, a Hittite, a babe not-in-the-woods. Remember, feed a man a fish, and he has eaten a fish. Teach a man how to fish and he can eat more fish, right up to when he limits out. You need to learn how to fish."

"Perhaps so. I've often thought that fly fishing would be enjoyable. It seems peaceful and amiable, other than it might not be such a pleasant experience for the fish. Eh?"

"There's nothing like it."

"I look forward to it. If you think we can fit it in."

"We can. We will. What else do you want to do? Levi and Loyal, the road warriors, turned fearless fisherman, in charge of our own destinies, all the time we need to do whatever we want."

His eyes roll upward, and I see the slightest of grins cross his features. I'd never quite believed that eyes could really twinkle. And then I saw Loyal's eyes do just that. Twinkle, sparkle, set off a little fire. He is thinking of something else.

"Tell me, Uncle Loyal. You can't hide it. I can tell by looking at you that you're thinking of something."

"Well, in North Dakota, we don't have many mountains."

"Like none."

"If you're a purist, I suppose you're correct. Like none."

"And so? Eh?" Good grief. I was developing a Dakota twang.

"I've always . . ." And here he stops, and he seems to be selecting his words carefully. "I've always wanted to do this. This one thing. Since I was a lad."

"And the one thing is?"

"Climb a mountain. A real mountain. Not just a hill, but a real mountain, something with snow on the top. A place where I could look down and see snow on my shoes. It would be most satisfying."

"You've never climbed a mountain? Uncle Loyal, we need to get you out more often!"

"My age."

"Age doesn't count. No worries. We'll find just the right mountain. Not too steep, but a real mountain. We'll take pictures of you on top of it. We'll find a flag, and you can pop it in and pose. We'll put you on YouTube. We'll get you your own Facebook page. Loyal Wing. Mountaineer. You'll be like Sir Edmund Hilltop or whatever that guy's name is, and I'll be like your faithful Sherpa guide. We will conquer that mountain."

"Do you think we can?"

"No doubt. *We can.*"

"A mountain?"

"Just the right kind of mountain."

"It sounds intriguing."

"When we get deeper into Montana, where there are more mountains. Catch some fish, hike a mountain. I will open new horizons to you. You've really led a sheltered life, Uncle Loyal. You've missed a few things by living on the flatlands."

"I would not disagree. Other than the war. Nothing too sheltered about that."

He pushes his feet forward and lets his back relax. His head tilts back on the car seat. He looks happy and pleased with himself and a little excited. This is going to be an amazing trip. The car lurches ahead, the air conditioning blowing on our faces. It is crazy and wonderful and exhilarating and fun all at once. Me, a twenty-four-year-old guy without hardly a lick of experience, and I am going to show Loyal something new in life. He'd given me a few things on this trip; now it was my turn to give something back.

The countryside zips by, more fields of wheat and corn, more prairie potholes shimmering in the hot morning sun. We see some rough country, up and down, red rimrock country, where no crops will grow. We pass through the little towns with their sturdy, agricultural-sounding names— Burlington, Berthold, Stanley, Ross, and Wheelock. We see the high-and-low, duck-like bob of oil well pumps dotting the landscape. We drop down toward the big, lazy Missouri River and then drive up a rise toward

Williston, flat and spread out, oozy green trees marking the edges of town. We find a restaurant in Williston, a hole-in-the-wall kind of place, where the people who work there all speak Spanish and fix us an awesome lunch of Mexican food.

And then we climb back into the car and push our way into Montana.

"Not far to go now. We should be at Glenn's in a little more than an hour," I say cheerily, filled with good food, the cool air blowing on my face, driving fast. "We're making good time. Really good time."

Uncle Loyal shifts his weight and doesn't say much in response. He is quiet again. It was probably the combination of heavy food and hot weather and a long day of driving.

"Glenn. You need to know something about him. I hope you're not disappointed in Glenn," he says.

"Can't be. He's a friend of yours, ergo a friend of mine. Nothing more to it than that. And think of what we have to look forward to after our visit there. Ergo, the mountains of Montana, fishing, hiking, climbing, cool temperatures, awesome views. Ergo, we'll be on top of the world, Uncle Loyal. I like the word *ergo* by the way, even though I don't know what it means. Ergo, bergo, slergo."

We drive on, farther into Montana. Uncle Loyal fidgets a bit. He looks out the window, beyond the grain fields, past the round-topped hills. He shuffles his feet and stretches. Although it's midday, a quarter moon hangs overhead in the summer sky.

We pass through an Indian reservation, then on to Glasgow, a small town with a wide main street, just north of a giant dam and reservoir. We push ahead. We near the place where Uncle Loyal said that Glenn was.

"Not far now. Can't be. Next stop: Glennville. Glenn, baby, here we come."

"Only a few miles," Uncle Loyal says slowly. "There's a small town just ahead. That's where we'll find him."

"Good. Let me know where I need to turn."

We drive in silence for twenty minutes. Then Uncle Loyal shifts in his seat, drums his fingers on the dash, and turns his head to look out the window. We pass a sign that gave the name of a small town—actually, less than a town, just a few homes, a grocery store, a grain elevator, a closed gas station, a building that advertised, "Antiques and Collectibles, No Junk," a bar, a large stone house that said, "Bed and Breakfast, Open, Call Ahead," but gave no phone number, and a large garage with a dozen old cars and trucks parked outside, a man dressed in greasy coveralls standing on the side of the highway.

Uncle Loyal says, "Here it is. Here is where Glenn is."

"Where is he?"

"Up there. On the little hill to the left. The green place." He flings his hand in a general direction to the south, toward a small green patch of grass surrounded by tall trees.

I look in the direction he pointed and squint. Something isn't right. I can't see any houses.

Then the bottom drops out of my stomach. The green place. Yes, of course. *Now I know.* It all comes to me, all of what Uncle Loyal said suddenly made sense. Of course he'd be at home. Glenn couldn't be anywhere else.

"It's a cemetery," I say.

He glances toward me sheepishly. "Yes."

"Uncle Loyal. That's where Glenn is, right?"

Uncle Loyal turns away. He now looks troubled, and I can just about guess the unspoken questions that are on his mind. "Does it matter, Levi? Do you understand? Will we still catch fish? Are you angry with me?"

His face is drawn. He fidgets uncharacteristically. He looks straight ahead.

"Yes. I'm sorry, Levi. I didn't tell you. I should have. I tried a couple of times, but I didn't think you would go all this way if you knew my friend Glenn wasn't alive. I should have said something more, been more adamant and forthcoming."

I slow down as we near the intersection. I'm trying to sort this out. It made no sense, and it made a lot of sense at the same time. I flip on my turn signal and wheel the red car to the left onto a dusty gravel road that led up the hill.

"I'm sorry," Uncle Loyal says. "I am truly sorry. But . . ." and he doesn't finish his sentence.

I slow more as we get to the entrance of the small country cemetery. The markers, all a light gray, stand in perfect lines.

I steal a glance at Uncle Loyal. I think, *He has no one, he has nothing, nothing but his wisdom and his stories and his experience living on the plains. His wife is gone, his friends are gone. He has two daughters, one he hardly hears from and the other who has given me a plastic card and six hundred bucks to get him to Utah so that she can feel better about the way she's treating him.* I feel a surge of sympathy or understanding or empathy or ethos or pathos or one of those words I should have learned in English 101 but never took the time.

But I feel *something*, and that's what counts, I suppose. I don't want him to be sad or unhappy or feeling that he let me down. I know what I *could* do, what I *should* do, what I *would* say. I take a gulp and feel I am on the edge of doing something that would be considered maybe as an act of kindness, and at the same time I hope it won't be clumsy. I have to admit that I have a bit of a record when it comes to being clumsy. I need more practice at being kind. It seems like the ideal time to start. Loyal's needs had become more important than mine.

"It's okay, Uncle Loyal," I say. Then I tell a lie. "I knew a hundred and fifty miles ago, even before we crossed the state line into Montana that Glenn wasn't alive. You dropped enough hints. It's okay. Really. I would've come anyway. I did come. Proves it, right?"

He doesn't say a thing but looks at me and gives me a slight nod. I know then things will be okay, and I also know he is embarrassed. I also know that these few minutes at that country cemetery in the middle of nowhere mean a lot to him. I stop the car. He gets out, slump-shouldered, and walks toward a marker on the far corner of the cemetery, near two tall cottonwood trees. I think it best to just watch him for a few minutes from afar.

I slide out of the car. I hear him say, "Hello, Glenn. It's been such a long time. I haven't been very good to you these last few years. My apologies, old friend. Have you heard I'm on my way to Utah?"

Then he turns toward me and beckons me to follow.

"Glenn, I want you to meet someone. He is important. He is special. Without him, I would not be here."

I take a few slow steps toward the grave, and when I get there, I look at Loyal, then look at the marker and say, "Pleased to make your acquaintance, Glenn. You have a good friend here in Loyal Wing."

And the funny thing is that I meant it.

Chapter Fifteen

From the Depths of the Valley
We Travel toward the Tops of Peaks

I MADE A SERIOUS MISTAKE. I did not take my great-nephew into my total confidence. I was not honest with him. I did not treat him as I should have. I did not tell him that Glenn, the closest friend I had, other than my Daisy, passed away seven years ago when a large stack of hay bales toppled over and crushed him. Yes, I tried, I made an attempt, but I stopped short of the mark.

My fear was this: Levi, young and in a hurry and obviously sent to North Dakota to pick me up and drive me to Utah for a sum of money, would not understand my deep friendship with Glenn Leuthold, would not understand how much it meant to me to visit his grave site in the cemetery for what may well be the last time in my life.

When will I be able to come back to this stark Montana Hi-Line country? The answer, I knew, was likely never.

So I engaged in this subterfuge. I never really told Levi that Glenn was dead, but I also never really told him he was alive. I chose my words carefully. I put it out of my mind how I would deal with Levi once the truth was known. Certainly, I would apologize. After visiting the cemetery, we could travel with haste toward Utah, we could drive straight through. It would not matter. I would owe at least that much to Levi for taking me so far out of his way.

But something happened on our way to Montana. Levi changed. He was a different young man than the one who picked me up less than two days ago. No longer in quite the hurry, no longer with mere dollar signs in his eyes and viewing me as a commodity, an object to be transported, but rather, as a human being deserving of attention and respect. This journey we are sharing, we are both growing from it, the result that most journeys inevitably cause.

He said to me, "I knew before we got to Montana that Glenn wasn't alive."

I asked how he knew.

He said, "You said something. You said, 'That's where we'll find him,' when I asked you where he lived. You didn't say, 'That's where he lives. His house is green and he lives on a farm and I hope we don't catch him when he's calling in the cows or feeding the chickens or cutting alfalfa.' You just said that's where we'll find him. You like to describe things. You notice colors and sounds and how things work. And then you said zero, zip, nada about Glenn's life, other than what happened a long time ago. That's a big clue, Uncle Loyal. You're not good at making up things or hiding things."

I didn't give him credit enough for intuition. But I still don't know if he really knew.

After we got out of the car, I called him over to the grave site. I know what he said. But . . . I watched carefully for clues. Was he angry with me? Was he impatient? Did he feel deceived? Did he feel used? I saw none of those signs. He quietly walked to the headstone. After a few minutes, I tell him more about Glenn.

I say to him, "Glenn was a true friend. That is a rare and precious thing. Even in the Church, we have many acquaintances for whom we feel love, but few friends we actually do love."

I say, "Glenn was a man of wisdom and experience."

I say, "Glenn was constant, like the Northern Star."

I say, "You would have liked Glenn."

Levi says, "I'm sure I would have."

We spend about a half hour there. I pull a few nearby weeds. Levi takes them from me, walks to the little custodian's building at the cemetery, really nothing more than a utility shed, and drops them into a plastic trash can. After that, he walks back to the car and stands quietly, allowing me to gather my thoughts and say a few quiet words to Glenn before heading back to the car. I know when it is time. I come back to the car and get in. Levi quietly drives away from the cemetery, and we head west again on Highway 2.

Finally, I say, "To Utah. As quickly as you choose to travel."

He says, "Yes, to Utah."

I am disappointed. For all that I had put him through, I harbored the faint hope and an opaque vision of hiking toward a snow-capped mountain, fishing pole in hand, laughing with one another in the brittle, piney mountain air.

Levi grips the steering wheel tighter and presses on the accelerator. We drive several miles in disquieting silence, past the tawny fields, the jade of cottonwood and box elder trees.

Then he says, "Do you think she's over me?"

Startled, I ask, "Who?"

The corners of his mouth pinch upward. "How soon you forget, Uncle Loyal. I am disappointed and disillusioned. I expected more from you. You know. Her."

"Her?"

"Yes, her."

The light dawns. "Ah. The motel clerk, the lovely one, Evelyn. She of the amazing hair."

"Of course. Yes. *She. Her. It.* My princess today, my future queen of tomorrow."

"Levi, I doubt she will ever forget you. You are one of a kind. You are unique."

He reaches over and playfully slaps the side of my knee and says, "That's what I wanted to hear. I miss Mr. Rogers telling me that there is no one else just like me." He sits back in the driver's seat and says, "Let's get out that map. We need to find us a mountain to climb."

"I believe I have located some to the south of here. It will mean turning away from Highway 2 and driving through the central part of the state. We likely will not get to the mountains until tomorrow."

"Just tell me where to turn. I'll do the rest. To the mountains."

"Yes, to the mountains."

If luck should smile upon me and if my traveling companion remained true, I might just yet end up with foggy blue breath and snow on my shoes before this trip was over.

CHAPTER SIXTEEN

IN OUR ROAMING, WE CAUSE
AUNT BARBARA WONDER AND SURPRISE

UNCLE LOYAL IS GETTING INTO the navigator's role big time. He unfolds the map about every half hour and studies it. He tells me he's looking for roads that will lead us to mountains. He tells me that he thinks the best roads are those that get squiggly and bunched because that must mean there are a lot of switchbacks and changes in elevation. He tells me he's looking for little dots of light blue, signifying lakes, and thin ribbons of slightly darker blue, which show where the streams and rivers are. And he also looked on the map for the little triangles with the name of a mountain and the number beside it signifying its elevation. He tells me with a laugh and more than a little excitement that there must be a thousand mountains in Montana higher than ten thousand feet.

He tells me to turn left when we reach the junction of Highway 191. He tells me that there are some mountains about twenty miles away, and while they don't appear to be tall or impressive, we might want to take a look at them. Scout them out, he says. Reconnoiter. Choose our path.

I make the turn, and we drive through hill country. A blue, hazy patch of pine green rises to the west. Mountains, for sure, but they aren't the kind we're after. We drive closer, and Uncle Loyal says, "The map says there's a little town at the foot of the mountains. It's going to be dark soon, and I don't see any other towns nearby. Maybe we can drive by and see if there's a place to eat, a place to sleep. We've put in a long day."

I agree with him. It *has* been a long day, and I am thinking that a soft bed somewhere sounds unbeatable. And maybe I'll meet another . . . another . . . let's see, my true love's name . . . Evelyn, yes, that's it, Evelyn, in the wilds of Montana, and I could get over my broken heart completely. Sew that aorta right up. Yes, sir, sounds good to me.

We make our way up a twisty two-lane road. The pavement turns a dark bluish-gray, and the sky fades from gold to orange to the same color as the road. I love this part of the day. It's sleepy, it's peaceful, it's quiet, and it's hard to tell the difference between colors. Everything blends. I always want to sing "Kumbaya" right about now. The world becomes muted. I don't think of money or what jobs my roommates landed this summer. I don't think of the grocery store. I don't think of getting ahead. I don't think of all the miles I have left to go.

Uncle Loyal stares out the window. We pass through a small canyon with a trickle of a stream coming down. We start to see old, little homes, more like cabins, on both sides of the road. Most of them are dark. We make a great, wide, sweeping curve in the road, and then ahead of us is the small town, not much more than a dozen buildings.

"Old mining town, played out. My suspicion," says Uncle Loyal. "We may not find a place to eat, and I am unsure of the quality of the food should we locate a restaurant." He pauses. "There. Over there. I see a sign that says café, and it looks as though it is open for business."

A sign flickers in the dim light. It reads, "Hardpan Café," and below it, in smaller letters, it reads, "and Hotel."

It was gray and dusky by then, and even though it is August, there is a chill in the air. We must have been five thousand feet up in the mountains. Uncle Loyal and I park headfirst outside the café and hotel and peer inside. There are no customers. In fact, there is only one man inside, a fellow with wild, gray, frizzy hair, dressed in overalls and leaning over a table reading a newspaper. I think, *This comes right out of an old, bad western movie. Bet anything his name is Snuffy or Grumpy or Dutch.*

"We need to ask ourselves a couple questions: How hungry are we? How tired are we? Do we take a chance on this place?" I mumble.

Uncle Loyal looks into the darkening sky. Stars are popping out. A little puff of wind floats down the canyon. I hear music from a radio drifting across the empty main street. Uncle Loyal strokes his chin thoughtfully. "We can try it. It may be quite the experience. It almost certainly will become a good story to tell. We are off the beaten path. Let's try it."

With more courage than I feel, I say, "Okay, let's head on in and give this place a shot, but I reserve the right to run out of the restaurant like a raving crazy rat, jump in the car, and drive away at a high rate of speed. And if you can't keep up with me, tough, Uncle Loyal."

"I agree to your conditions. However, I must insist on a head start."

We push through the door, which has a little bell attached to it. The tinkling of the bell causes the man at the table to raise his head and take a long look at us.

"You got a couple of customers, Libby. Live 'uns. First since last March, just after the blizzard, I reckon. Better come in a hurry, 'fore they git scared and run out a here."

"Quaint Montana humor," I whisper to Uncle Loyal. "Local color."

A small woman comes from the kitchen, short, hunched over, wrinkled, but with a smile that made the place almost seem normal. She does not, however, have very good hair.

"All I can feed you is eggs, hotcakes, or a cheeseburger," she says. "All's we got left. It's fresh, though. Mostly. Eggs keep a long time."

Uncle Loyal says he'll take the eggs and hotcakes, and I order the cheeseburger.

The short story is that the meal is fine, the old timer comes our way and talks to us as we eat, and Libby, the chief cook, waitress, and owner, eventually comes over, puts her elbows on the table, and joins in the conversation. We sit there, plastic table cloth, plastic flowers in a plastic yellow vase, and talk as if we are all old friends. We get the history of the place—an old mining town, the tailings polluted by arsenic, the water dangerous to drink, and the air filled with unhealthy dust. Other than that, it is a fine place, Libby and Dutch—or Bill or Sourdough or whatever his name was—reassure us.

"Not a bad place for kids, other than the arsenic in the water," Dutch astutely points out. "Makes the kids' faces stick in one place. Stunts their growth too. We got nothin' but little biddy kids here."

Uncle Loyal whispers, "More quaint mountain humor, I assume."

"The feds are pouring a lot of money into this old wreck of a town," Libby says. "But I don't know. Just don't know. I think we're done for. What few kids we have don't stick around, and you can't get nowhere without your young." She drums her knuckles on our table, distracted by the thought and glancing around the little restaurant, which is where, she probably figured, she was going to die. I feel sorry for her. She is a nice woman.

Eventually, Uncle Loyal gets around to asking if any rooms upstairs are for rent. Libby says yes, all singles, shared bathroom, clean, and how does twenty dollars cash sound for the night?

Uncle Loyal says, "It sounds just about right."

Libby says, "Well, it's about time to clean up the place. If you want, breakfast will be served starting about six, maybe seven," if she woke up tired. We understood that was our signal to get our suitcases and bags and head upstairs.

"Take whichever room you want, none of them are locked, and you don't need to lock them here. You won't be bothered," Libby said. The old man in overalls reached over to Libby, gave her a little kiss on her ear, and said, "Good night, babe. See you in the morning."

Libby looks both pleased and annoyed and tugs at his hand and squeezes it. Uncle Loyal and I walk to the car, get our belongings, and march upstairs. He takes room six; I tromp into room five. They are plain and old and don't smell quite okay, but the bed in my room seems fine, and the sheets and blankets are, as Libby promised, clean and crisp.

I clean up for the night in the common bathroom. Then I get back to my room, climb into the slightly creaky bed, stare at the ceiling, and begin to take inventory, something that usually doesn't make sleep come any faster.

Where did this day go?

Why was it so important for Uncle Loyal to visit Glenn's grave site?

Will the room light up the next time I see Rachel?

What did I see today? The plains, the hills, a few mountains, old people, young people, people with brown skin in the Mexican restaurant, the food they cooked so well. A town that was dying. A good cheeseburger in a place where you shouldn't drink the water. Blue mountains, blue sky, green forest, all fading to a gray in the twilight. And now here, this room, this place, by myself, Uncle Loyal probably snoozing next door. A promise to climb a mountain, teach an old man how to fish for trout. A sunset that went from brilliant yellow to lush red to drowsy purple.

A fast red car that I slowed down. A woman with big hair, big hair that she loved. The fleeting flash and pop of Rachel's face before me when I told Uncle Loyal about her. The fuzzy, finicky, flustered feeling I had when I thought about her. An old man in overalls, who called an old woman "babe." That old woman who could really cook.

It had been quite a day. My thoughts were diffused, gauzy, pleasant. Uncle Loyal, who thought I'd be upset about the detour to Glenn's grave. Uncle Loyal, so wise, so pleasant . . .

My cell phone chimes, a foreign sound in this place, a noise that seems loud and raucous. I reach over for it in my bag. I look at the display. It's Aunt Barbara calling. I flip it open and put it up to my ear.

"Hello?"

"Levi. Barbara Bates here."

I didn't like that beginning. Of course I know it's Barbara. Of course I know it's Barbara Bates. What about Aunt Barbara? Or your friend Barbara? She gets to the point quickly.

"How are you? Where are you? Did you pick up my father okay? Is he okay? You know, is he going to *be* okay?"

"Your dad's fine. We're doing fine. We're somewhere in a little town in the mountains of northern Montana. At least, I think we're in Montana. I don't know for sure. No. Wait. Yeah, must be Montana. You kind of lose track of time up here."

"Where? Northern Montana? That's so out of the way. Remember, I'm in the travel and hospitality business. I thought you'd be much closer to Bountiful. I *hoped* you would be."

"Yeah, it is out of the way, but not too much, and your dad wanted to see an old friend, and I had the time to take him, so I thought, why not?"

"Which old friend?"

"Oh, I can't remember his name. Nice old fellow though. Maybe his name was Gary or Mitch or something like that. Didn't have much to say. Quiet, for sure. Not a real ball of fire, but he and your dad got along super, and it was worth the extra time to take the detour. Not what I'd call a great personality—couldn't get him to say a thing—but they were happy to see each other. Hardly even knew he was there. But Uncle Loyal was excited to be around him again. Really excited. It meant a lot to him. I met him too; we had a quick chat."

I'm babbling. I wish I had a babbling filter. But I'm covering for Uncle Loyal.

Silence. She's thinking. Then, slowly, the judgment. "I guess that's all right."

"And I made some promises to Uncle Loyal. He's never fished for trout in a mountain stream. Not ever. Just pond stuff in North Dakota. So I start thinking. Here we are in Montana, the Big Sky, and streams about every five miles where the trout almost jump out of the creek and into your lap, so I told him, 'Loyal, we'll do some fishing while we're here.'"

"Fishing? Why? My father is old for that. I'm not sure that's a good idea. Why, Levi?"

"Because we are here, and he wants to, and this place is crazy with streams and lakes with lots of fish. That's why." I almost say, "And before you put him in jail, it would be a nice experience for him," but fortunately, my good sense made a rare appearance just in time.

Jangling. The jangling of precious metal on her arms, around her neck, down her wrists. The jangling that let me know, seven hundred miles away and in a whole different world, that she has *money.* The jangling of her thoughts as I told her something that was beyond the scope of her everyday world. The jangling of emotions as she thought about her father somewhere in tall mountains with icy cold clear water rushing down a gully with a fishing rod in his hands.

"Don't you need fishing gear? And a license?"

"Oh, sure. But the card you gave me. I could charge a couple of cheap rods and buy the licenses, just a day license, and we could go fishing, and you'd have one happy pappy when he arrives in Utah. We'll bring you a fish. A delicious fresh trout."

"Fishing."

"Yes, fishing."

"How much will it all cost?"

"I don't know. Maybe a hundred. A little more."

"I don't know."

"Take it off what you owe me. I think he'd have a hoot. Look, Aunt Barbara, it's something he *wants* to do. This is kind of his last fresh breath, his last chance, most likely. Take the money off what you owe me, if that's why you're worried."

Ping! *Levi*, I thought, *you just shot the arrow straight into her.* I could almost sense her backbone stiffening across the cell towers for miles and miles. Her voice takes on the slightly offended air of the nouveau riche. More jangling, and I promise I can smell the creamy, fruity, blossom-of-some-sort perfume that she wears, the stuff that made me think of orange creamsicles.

"It's not the money," she says, which pretty much confirmed to me it was mostly about the money. "I'm just worried. He's my father, you know. What if he falls and breaks a hip or something?"

"From what I've seen of your dad, he'd probably say, 'Levi, I beg your pardon, but it seems I have fallen in the stream. It seems that my hip is broken and my mobility hampered somewhat. May I obtain your assistance to help me to the shore, eh? And from there, perchance, to the hospital, if it is not too much of an imposition? Thank you.' That's about what he'd say. Aunt Barbara, he's the most polite human being I've ever been around. He's from North Dakota. He's tougher than I am and probably in better shape."

"Well . . ." And there is a pause. Another *long* pause. I knew I had put more on her plate than she expected. "Go ahead, then. Keep the receipts. I can write it off. And keep the fish, too. Heaven knows I don't want a three-day-old fish. One hundred dollars?"

"Maybe two hundred."

"Two hundred. Oh. That much. Oh well. Do it, then."

"I will."

"Call me. Let me know how he does. Fishing. Oh my. This is a twist I didn't expect."

"It'll be fine, it's all good, Aunt Barbara. He'll be safe. I'll watch every move he makes, every step he takes, every breath he takes, I'll be watching him, and I think I'm sounding like an old song."

"You are. I think you're nuts, Levi. I wish I knew you were nuts before I asked you to do this. I thought you were more normal than this. More solid. But you're insane. Just be careful."

"I will, and actually, I enjoy being nuts. Uncle Loyal kind of brings it out in me."

"Well, okay. Good night, Levi. And thank you. For what you're doing for my dad. This isn't quite what I had in mind, but I know you'll take care of him."

"You can count on that. I'm enjoying the trip. The road trip. Uncle Loyal and Little Levi's most wonderful journey."

"Good night, Levi."

"Good-bye, Aunt Barbara."

Score! Score one for Levi. I'd passed the Barbara stiff acid cynical hardboiled test. *And I got her to pay for it.* I can hardly wait to see Uncle Loyal and tell him the good news. Score one for being spur-of-the-moment. Score one for being impetuous. Score one for all the little people in the world who want to do something crazy and then decide they can't just because it is crazy, and they wonder what other people will think and say and who will talk about it and how they'll be judged. *Score one for freedom.* The freedom of humankind. I click off my cell phone and clip it shut in the happy haze of triumph. Just what victory I had won, I couldn't quite pinpoint, but I knew I had won something, and it was important, and it felt good. *Score!*

As it turned out, I didn't have long to wait to see Uncle Levi. The little voice in the back of my head reminds me that I have not brushed my teeth. I tell the little voice to go away, I am tired, and I don't want to go down the hall to the shared bathroom to brush my teeth. The little voice turns into a big voice and reminds me that I'd had orthodontics, and it meant my family didn't go on a vacation for two years, and that if I don't brush my teeth, even if the water here is bad, they might all chip and fall out and I'll have nothing left but gums in the morning, and my mother would cry when she saw me, and my dad would never allow me in a family photograph again. Then the little voice, in fact, starts sounding just like my mom.

With that, the little-voice-turned-big-voice wins, and I sit up on the bed, fumble around for my Big Bird toothbrush and toothpaste, and thump down to the bathroom.

Uncle Loyal is there, in his plaid pajamas. He's brushing his teeth. He seems not to notice me, although I'm sure he does, since it isn't like there are dozens of other people in this small room. His hand moves up and down, the brushing like a slow metronome. He slowly, mechanically, finishes brushing his teeth, then rinses his mouth and turns toward me. He looks at me for a full five seconds. He seems to be searching for thoughts and the right words to express them.

"Levi. My thanks to you."

Simple words are best.

"You're welcome, Uncle Loyal. Good night."

"Good night."

With that, he half waddles by me and turns to go to room six.

I think, *I can hardly wait until tomorrow.*

CHAPTER SEVENTEEN
IF YOU SLAP THE WATER WITH YOUR LINE, THE FISH WILL HEAR YOU AND NOT RISE TO THE FLY

I SAW LEVI JUST BEFORE retiring. It was in the common bathroom. He entered while I was brushing my teeth. He seemed a little reluctant to interrupt me, so he just stood quietly while I finished. Then I told him thank you. It seemed the right thing to say, for driving me, for not being annoyed or peevish about our side trip to visit Glenn's grave. And there's more. He had spoken enthusiastically about fishing and climbing mountains, and I believe we will attempt to do both on this strange journey to my destination. It may sound odd, but I really do want to fish and hike and see places that I will never see again. The thought of me wiggling my toes in a snowbank in mid-August appeals to me more than most would understand. I come from the plains. Do you know what a treat a late-summer clump of snow underfoot would be for me?

He told me, "You'll love to fish. We'll fish tomorrow, Uncle Loyal. We'll catch some fat trout, and then we'll show the world what good guys we are. We'll let them go. Catch and release. They can go back to their deep pools and tell all their buddies about it. Their close encounters with humans. All the fish will want to hear their story."

Then he said, "You're welcome. Good night. Sweet dreams," and I left.

I climb into bed. The long fingers of dark blue and gray had stretched down the sides of the mountains, through the gullies and washes, and firmly clasped this little town that will be my home for a night. Sleep comes easily for me. I see my girls when they were little. I see Daisy when she was young. I dream of Glenn. I dream of my home. And in the morning, all my dreams having run their course and planted their thoughts, having lifted me as though I were in the hands of angels, I awake, ready for what this new day will bring.

As it turned out, it brought me a lot.

I hear Levi in the hallway a little after seven. I had been awake for an hour but decided to rise when he began to rustle. We go downstairs together and find the irrepressible Libby hard at work by her grill, a restaurant full of people, mostly old, mostly men, most of whom look as if they'd known hard work in the mines with little reward and less still to show for it. She brightens when she sees us.

"Sleep okay? Good. We've got sausage and eggs and toast, and that's about it. Maybe a little orange juice. I'll fix you gents up in a heartbeat. No coffee, eh?"

The breakfast is delicious. The stories, in snitches of conversation, are humorous and good-natured, slightly raucous, and it strikes me that these people who worked deep under the surface of the earth had a bond and a feeling for each other that went beyond mere friendship. We pay Libby, who also ran the cash register, for breakfast and for the two rooms. "Thirty bucks will do it. I know what I said last night, but I'm not in this motel business for money; I'm in it for the people I get to meet and help. I like you fellows. Come back and see us."

And then Levi and I are on the road, leaving the small, dying, mountain mining town in the early morning light.

A few miles closer to the Glad Tidings Assisted Living Home with each passing hour, I think.

We drive south. Bigger mountains in that direction, the map seemed to tell me. I don't want to ask Levi about fishing, but I hope he remembers; I hope he was earnest. We drive across plains, big monstrous seas of wheat or alfalfa, but in the distance, no matter where you look, the mountains shimmer in the hot sun of the morning, beckoning.

I thought of the streams that must come tumbling down the mountainsides, the lakes cupped gently near the tops of their slopes. I thought of the fish, content, cool in their watery homes, living in the deep parts of a creek or lake, under a rock shelf, or in the fizzy roil of a rapid. I thought of God and how much He planned and His unabashed brilliance to dream up and then create a world where men and fish could both thrive in atmospheres as wildly different as liquid and land.

Levi says to me, "I talked with Barbara last night. She wanted to know how we were doing."

"And what message did you give her? I also would like your assessment of how we are doing."

He takes his eyes off the road ahead and looks at me, a grin, pure and boyish, and says, "I told her we were doing great and that we were going to go fishing today. She liked that idea. It took a little convincing, but she came around. She's worried that you're going to fall and I'll have to pack you out on my back or something like that, but I told her it was more likely the other way around. I'd fall and crack my head open, and you'd strap me on your shoulders and haul me out. I think that made her feel better."

"If that happened, we'd find a way. But it won't happen. We will be fine. We will triumph in the mountains," I tell him.

"We need gear. We need to find a place and pick up everything. We could be fishing by the end of today, or tomorrow morning. That soon. But we need to keep our eyes open for a place that could sell us some gear."

I am happy to hear that fishing is still paramount in his plans. I looked forward to it. When you are old, you look forward to the things, small and large, that give you hope. Ten years ago, it would have been adding another grandchild or celebrating a baptism. Ten years ago, it would have been looking ahead to a long span of many years with my Daisy.

But our hopes change, and sometimes they diminish and sometimes they go away, and then our hope becomes our hope: we hope that a new hope will sprout, send a tender green shoot from brown earth, and find a way to stretch toward sunlight and flourish. From sharing a long life with Daisy and then to her passing, my hopes had changed and now centered on a place called Glad Tidings and that it would not be too stifling and eventually suffocate me; and in the near-term, that I could go fishing in a Rocky Mountain creek. That, and the allure of some kind of salvation, are about the only hopes left to me. And one more hope: the hope I am beginning to feel for Levi.

That, and the hope that I would go fishing today, or tomorrow, and then maybe go again. Utah has mountains, I told myself. Utah has streams and lakes. Therefore, Utah must have fish. I would find out.

I feel sleepy. I had wanted to stay awake and alert on this drive, keep my great-nephew company, prove to him, and to myself, that I could be a good companion. The pearl-blue skies, the gentle rhythm of driving down the state highway, the warm-but-not-hot temperature in the car. My thoughts drift pleasantly. The little mountain town and the plucky cook, cashier, waitress, and proprietor Libby; the visit to Glenn's grave site; Levi telling Barbara I would be fine in the mountains.

And then I am asleep. And my dreams come to me again.

I dream of my daughters. I dream they are young, small enough for me to hold in my arms, to toss them gaily in the air and catch them amid their laughter of delight. I dream that Daisy and I are young, too, that the townsfolk peer in the windows of my pharmacy, then become my customers and later become my friends. I dream of the hand-lettered signs that Daisy had made that I hung in the pharmacy's windows announcing specials and the opening and closing hours, the one in black block letters, "In an emergency, call . . ." with my home phone number listed. I dream of the gentle Dakota days in the springtime, when the breeze came from the northwest, the air clean and smelling fresh, and the sting of winter fading fast. I dream that those days, those times, will last forever and nothing will change.

And in the middle of these dreams, I see myself in a mirror, the mirror on our own armoire, just inside our bedroom door in the brown house. And I hear myself say, "Do you see? Do you see it all now? These dreams are your hope, they have been forever. You have more hope than you realize, Loyal Wing." And all of these thoughts and dreams lift me.

How long I had waited to have my dream at hand, to be on the earth, with my family.

Daisy and my daughters, a good life, managing to stay true to what I felt and what I believed in. Yes, those were my dreams and, I suppose, my dreams came true, and now my dreams were my stories.

Somewhere in the filminess of my world of half sleep, I hear the car engine slow, the click of a turn signal, the sound of our tires turning off the blue highway. With labor, I lift my eyes and see that we are in a very large parking lot with a very large store in front of us.

I say, "Why are we here, Levi? I have been asleep. I meant to keep you company. But I fell asleep. I am sorry. I apologize. Why are we here?"

He says, "We are here to buy fishing gear."

"Oh."

My voice, a little dry and a little flat, must have told him more than my single-word response. In that single word, *oh*, there was much.

"Something not right about that?"

"Well."

"Something's not right."

"It's just that . . . that this is a large store and sells many items. There must be a small store that sells just to fishermen. It would be run by a man named Stan or Herb, and he would know every fishing place for miles around. I think we need to find Stan or Herb."

"You don't like the big-box stores, do you?"

"Not much. I have my reasons."

"Let me guess," my great-nephew says, his business acumen on the rise, his fingers wrapping around my thoughts and pulling them toward him. "Your pharmacy. I bet one of these big stores helped drive you right out of business. Put it smack under the old prairie sod. Am I right? Tell me I'm right. Of course I'm right."

"What you say could very well be true. At least in part. Daisy was beginning to feel ill. That was part of it too. And it was time, just time, I knew that. Few decisions are made based on only one factor."

"Okay. Look. I'm going to stop here, but only long enough to either ask someone where I could find a tackle shop named Stan's or look something up in the phone book. This is a decent-sized town. We could wander around all day and not find it. Let's take a shortcut. Fair enough?"

"Fair enough."

He slows the car, pulls to a stop, and hops out. I see him nearly accost a young man about his own age, gesture recklessly toward me, and jabber away. The stranger smiles knowingly and, in turn, makes motions with his right arm, which loosely translated, seems to mean, "Drive down this street for so long, turn at a light after a while, take a left after a block, and you will find Stan's Fish and Bait Shop on the next corner, across the street from a filling station."

Levi and the young man grin at each other, give each other a dangling slap of a handshake and brush of knuckles, and he returns.

"Stan's is only a couple of miles from here. The kid said it was the best place in the state to find gear. Only it's not called Stan's."

I'm mildly disappointed.

"It's called Chuck's."

I feel brighter. "Stan's, Herb's, Chuck's. All the same to me."

"Me, too. I'm with you. In the groove, Uncle Loyal. Let's go buy some gear."

We find Chuck's with no trouble. It was, from what I could tell, a fine shop devoted primarily to fishing gear. Levi obviously knows the sport. He strides up and down the four aisles of Chuck's, quickly dismissing some items, taking short, intense looks at others, making split-second decisions on all we would need. Clearly, he's an aficionado. Clearly, he has a good eye and keen judgment in all matters of mountains, clear flowing water, and stream fishing.

Our cache grows. Fishing poles—rods, Levi called them—an assortment of line, fishing flies, reels, and a large pair of rubbery long boots that he calls waders.

"I'll let you wear the waders. You can walk right into the stream, get to the best hole, cozy right on up to Mr. Trout. I've got these long shorts, and they dry out fast. I don't mind getting wet."

He stops for a moment, looks at me with his dark eyes, and simply says, "I love this."

He walks briskly to the front of the store, our bounty in hand. We purchase two five-day fishing licenses as well. The total comes to well more than three hundred dollars. Levi doesn't blink. He hands the yellow credit card to the clerk, a young man whose name tag reads, "Jason," who affably rings up the purchase.

"So where would you go if you were in our place—my grandfather here and me, generally heading to Utah, but we wanted to fish Montana along the way. Creek or small lake, something that we can wade into. Nothing difficult. Nothing too far out of the way. Gramps, here, has never been fly fishing."

Interesting, I think, that I had been elevated from Great-Uncle Loyal to Grandfather Loyal. I take it as a promotion. I nod agreeably toward the young man, Jason, who is eying me with the knowing look of an experienced appraiser of mountain fisherman potential.

He probably was thinking this: An old, round man with an oval face. Not in the best physical condition. Little hair, so he must wear a hat. Somewhat short legged, he should steer clear of water with boulders or swift currents. His age, seventies, maybe early eighties. A greenhorn in the mountains. No stiff hikes, not far from the road. Ah, the place. I have just the place. And then he said those very words.

"I have just the place," says the sagacious one, Jason. "I've got a map. I'll show you. Less than two hours from here. In one of the most beautiful mountain areas in the country. Up on the Beartooth Pass."

"Beartooth. Beartooth. I like the name," Levi bubbles. "Cool. Are there bears up there?"

"Bunches. Grizzlies, black bears. All over the place. You gotta be careful, or you can end up lunch for a bear."

"Excellent! I love this state."

Excellent is not the word I had in mind, but I think, at my age, meeting my demise at the jaws or paws of a grizzly bear probably would be preferable to meeting my demise at the hand of a disease that chewed away my bones and organs while I lay blank-faced and chalky in the Glad Tidings facility. And perhaps it *was* excellent in Levi's world. After all, if

Mr. Bear should show up in our pursuit of Mr. Trout, hungry and slavering and testy, Levi needed only to outrun me, a feat he would most assuredly accomplish without so much as breaking a sweat. And the scene was not without some humor as it passed by me, this encounter of men and bear, fishing poles flying, and a mad scramble toward wherever safety might be.

For Levi the torment was tornadoes. For me it might be a hulking bear. I like it. So I nod and say, "Yes. Excellent," to the approving looks of my young companions.

Jason and Levi get down to specifics. Take this highway there. Look for a dirt road in such-and-such a place. Follow it about a mile. Watch for a trailhead marker. Bear to the left at the first fork, to the right at the second. Walk ahead another hundred yards, and the creek comes tumbling down the hillside, and it's not large and has good holes, and the trout will be biting because it is not even close to a full moon and rain hasn't fallen in a week. Levi soaks this all in, his eyes fiery with excitement, his head bobbing up and down, almost feverish in his enthusiasm, an intermittent "Yes, yes, yes" and "Okay, okay, got it" punctuating Jason's instructions. He ends by telling us a good place to stay. "Way out there, off the beaten track, for sure, but the cabins are cool, and if you mention my name, they'll cut you a break on the price."

The transaction and the talk come to an end. Jason and Levi exchange an elaborate handshake, consisting of slaps and knuckle punches and fist grazing, brothers now and forever, brought together by time and circumstance and the love of the mountainous watery world where trout dwell. Jason wishes us good fishing and beseeches us to come again.

I turn as Levi and I push our way toward the door and ask, "Who is Chuck? Is he the owner of this store?"

Jason grins slyly. "There is no Chuck. I'm the owner, but I figured that not many people would come to a fly shop named Jason's."

With that, he reaches into a nearby bin and takes out a floppy, blue-brimmed hat and tosses it to me.

"You'll need this up there, Grandpa. Lots of sun. No charge. Good luck."

Levi winks at me, and we walk back to the shiny red car simmering in the sun.

"First we stop at a grocery store and get the basics of life. Chips, water, juice, and jerky. Lots of jerky. You can live off a bite of jerky for days. Boy Scouts. I learned it there."

So we stop by a grocery store, and Levi is in and out in less than five minutes. He comes back with four bags of food, two of which are completely filled with jerky. "I went back for a second bag," he tells me solemnly. "Can't ever have too much jerky."

The rest of that day passes pleasantly and mostly uneventful. We stop and have lunch at a small restaurant: chicken salad sandwich for me, Levi partaking of a roast beef sandwich with double fries and a tall milkshake. He chatters endlessly about fishing and our good fortune to have met up with the redoubtable Jason.

"That Jason, he's a good man. A real good man. Took to us both, told us the primo places to fish. Not everyone would do that. Most people who are really into it don't tell you their best places. But I think he was straight with us. That was a break. A big break, Uncle Loyal."

With that, he happily sucks up the last of his milkshake, making a loud gurgling sound through his straw. "Let's go. Let's get close to those mountains. Tomorrow, we fish."

We point the car first to the west, then to the south.

I keep my eyes on the low-slung ridge of blue-gray mountains to the south as we pass through the sleepy small towns of southern Montana with their fading main streets and architectural styles of bygone days.

With each passing mile, the mountains seem to grow larger and more imposing. An hour into our afternoon drive, I begin to see. I begin to understand these tall sentinels of the valley, how steep they were, their old rugged faces gouged and chiseled by millennia of wind, rain, frost, and snow. They seem to beckon me, as one old friend to another. "Come," they said. "Come and see us, Loyal. We will show you, old man, who we are, and you will show us who you are. We have both survived a good long time in our respective spheres; we have weathered what has come our way. Our faces are those of character. We understand each other. We know of each other's secrets. We all are cracked, and we show the strain of our time, of what we have experienced. But we are not broken. We are made of stone."

The mountains begin to look brighter as we drive closer. They take on the fine sheen of a pine green as the timber on their slopes takes form before my eyes. I feel a jolt of excitement as we get closer to the tall, solemn, wise mountains.

Levi talks on, talks on and on as we get closer, about fishing flies, matching the hatch and fishing tales and how he once got a big fish and how he let some other big ones get away. He tells me about turning back some fish and casting his line until it was dark outside on many occasions. He says that if you slapped the water with your line, the fish would hear it and they wouldn't bite. I nod. I'm only half paying attention as he rambles on about men and fish.

"Uncle Loyal? Are you listening to me?" he finally asks.

"Yes, yes. Of course, Levi. I'm listening. It's all very pleasant," I say. "The drive, these mountains, good company. I'm eager to get into these mountains. I have lived on flat land my whole life. It is time to see the sunrise or the sunset from another point of view."

We drive to the base of the mountain range and begin looking for the side road that will take us to the cabins that Jason told us about. After a great, curving bend in the two-lane highway, a stream rushed into view, and for some reason I was comforted. Here was proof that nature had worked her miracle—the combining of elevation, clouds, rain, snow, sun, and gravity gave the stream life. Only a God could think of it and make it thus. And it all came to this—clear, fast water dancing over rocks in a blind rush toward the valley.

And in that blind rush, certainly, there were fish. Their world, our world. Different worlds among us.

I am a flatlander, I remind myself. *I am a man of the prairie. This world is a new world to me.* I want to enter it. "New worlds," I say softly, so softly that Levi doesn't hear me as our car rumbles down the road. New worlds at our fingertips.

I think of Daisy, which I often do when I am about to experience something new.

Then I look up at the mountains, most of them cresting beyond ten thousand feet in the now-golden early evening sky, snow still lying in the deep, craggy pillows in the highest elevation. Mountains, I think. Mountains.

Excellent.

Tomorrow I would be among them.

CHAPTER EIGHTEEN

FISH. WE ARE FISH.
THEY ARE FISH. WE ALL ARE FISH

THAT JASON, HE WAS AWESOME. We connected. We bonded. He even gave us a tip on where we could stay: a cabin, away from the highway and the tourists and the summer rush of old people with bad legs in loud shorts and young parents looking stressed and little kids running everywhere out of control. Then he said he'd call ahead—the guy who owned it was a friend of his, someone named Marty—and that he'd make sure we had a place to stay, even if it was in Marty's house.

Marty was ready for us. He was a silver-haired man, trim as a triathlete, with blue eyes and a nice way with words. He greeted us as if we were long-lost buddies, showed us to one of the clean little cabins and told us to enjoy ourselves. He asked how long we planned to stay, and Uncle Loyal piped right up and said, "Oh, two days, most likely, but more if the fishing is sound." Marty smiled at that, and I could tell he was digging Uncle Loyal.

The sun was dipping behind those tall, rugged mountains, and my favorite time of the day in my favorite time of the year is at hand. The shadows are long, the air crisp and fresh smelling. The wind shuffles through the trees, and the best feeling of all, that wisp of chilly air, whirls down the canyon. It causes me to shiver. I know I will sleep well tonight.

I also know I'm hungry. Lunch seemed like a long time ago.

"Where would you go to grab dinner, Marty?"

"What are you in the mood for, amigo?"

It was the easiest question I'd been asked in a long time. "Meat. Red meat. I need meat. Thick, drippy red meat."

Of course, I hadn't talked over the subject of dinner with Uncle Loyal. I didn't know what he had in mind. But a big old beefsteak with a gob of mashed potatoes sounded perfect to me. Filling. Very western. Fitting. Very manly.

"Well, there's a place not far from here, my friend. Howie's, not much to look at, not much for atmosphere, but they have the best steaks between here and Denver. Only the locals really know about it. Incomparable T-bones. Heavenly prime rib. If meat is what you want, Howie's is where you need to be. As I said, a little rough hewn, but an unforgettable stop for a steak lover."

"Perfect."

Marty gives me directions, and a half hour later, after a ten-mile drive, we pull into the dusty parking lot of a roadside grill with a red neon light blinking, "Howie's for Steak."

I see a bunch of big motorcycles in the parking lot, all in a line. A couple of men, huge guys with bandannas, stare at us when we pull in. That should have been a clue. We were not in for a Relief Society kind of dinner at Howie's. Blue smoke curls up from a small chimney.

Uncle Loyal raises an eyebrow.

"Are you sure this is the place? It looks to be, I would venture, on the shady side. And I'm not much of a red-meat eater. I wonder if they have chicken. Or a nice Caesar salad."

"Marty said it was the best place for steak in the entire country, if not the world and universe. These places, they have *character*. It's the ambience. It's local culture. It's what makes them stick out. It gives them atmosphere. Besides, what are they going to do? Not serve us? Beat us up? Make us dance in pink tutus? This, Uncle Loyal, is part of the western experience. Remember, we are mountain men who will walk upon the turf of grizzlies tomorrow. What can these guys do to us? We'll be fine. Let's go."

He shrugs his shoulders and says softly, "As you wish."

We walk into the restaurant. Or bar. Or both. Or something. It's filled with a smoky gray haze and loud music, and the air smells sweet and funny. It takes my eyes a few seconds to adjust. When they do, I'm taken aback. Describing the place as "rough hewn" was generally equivalent to saying that Frankenstein could use a face-lift. The crowd, and it was a crowd, not customers, not a clientele, more like a mob, all sort of swings around to look at us. It seemed that every available inch of bare flesh—of which there was way too much—was adorned by a tattoo. Every earlobe, eyebrow, and most lips had wondrous displays of body piercings, and there appeared to be only two clean-shaven people in the entire business establishment, me and Uncle Loyal, a generalization that carried over to some of the female patrons.

Not that I was going to point out that fact to anyone there.

So there we stand, Uncle Loyal and me. I have on khaki shorts and a T-shirt with a cute little blue sailboat on it and sandals with no socks.

Uncle Loyal, chilled by the evening mountain air, had buttoned up a beige cardigan sweater over his plain white shirt and dark blue trousers.

There we were. Peter Pan and Tinkerbell. Squared up, face-to-face with the mob, in a biker bar. I wonder how long it had been since Marty had actually stepped inside this place.

I whisper to Uncle Loyal, trying not to move my lips or show my white teeth, "We're in a biker bar. These guys are in a motorcycle gang. Call me crazy, but I don't think anyone here has a temple recommend."

In the midst of this gigantic stare down, Uncle Loyal smiles and perkily says, "Good evening, ladies and gentlemen. Quite a lovely sunset outside."

I wanted to somehow slip through a crack in the old wood floor. How could we squirm through this mess? We could turn and run, although I had doubts about Uncle Loyal's ability to make a break for the red car, and I couldn't leave him behind, although I did feel a nanosecond's worth of temptation to do just that.

What I took to be a waitress—oh, how I missed my sweet Evelyn with her big hair, her thick makeup, the jangling of a single set of hoop earrings the size of hubcaps, the fairly sick smell of her cheap, heavy perfume— saunters up to us, and with a sly smile asks, "What'll it be for you boys? Come to get a little something to eat?"

I glance around again. The din of only a minute ago had all but disappeared. I'm not kidding: someone slapped the jukebox, and it stopped playing. This was like a bad scene in a bad western movie. I gulp. Make it good, Levi. Or this could be your last supper. This is a place where knives were used to cut meat but were also occasionally, I guessed, inserted between someone's ribs. What did I just say to Uncle Loyal? They won't beat us up? I wasn't so sure now.

I lower my voice and take my best shot at a Clint Eastwood growl.

"Yeah. Me 'n Pete here want meat. A big old piece of red meat. Can you fix us up?"

She eyes me again, top to toes, with what seems to be X-ray vision. I wish the little blue sailboat on my T-shirt would take on water and sink. I wish my legs were hairier and my voice deeper. I wish I had a scar on the side of my nose and breath bad enough to drop a horse a quarter mile away.

"We might be able to do that. Depends."

Depends? Depends on what? How could you walk in to a restaurant and ask for a meal and the waitress says, "Depends"? It was time for quick thinking. It was time to get culturally acclimatized in about one thumpy heartbeat. I look at Uncle Loyal. He is taking in the whole scene, smiling sweetly. He nods at the stiff, ugly, mean faces and then goes into his plains-polite mode again. "We understand the food here is wonderful. I hope you have low-cal dressing."

This is not the time, Uncle Loyal! This is not the place! I wanted to die. No, check that. I thought I would die. I had to change the subject. I had to change the feeling, the atmosphere, and I had to do it quickly. Manly. I needed manly fast.

"Well, see here, Miss. Me 'n Pete here, we like our meat rare. Once over the flame, and that's just about perfect. We like it so that it's just this side of mooing."

"Actually, I prefer chicken, if it's on the menu," Uncle Loyal chirps.

The waitress/gatekeeper/head thug either didn't hear him or ignored him. In any case, I'm relieved.

"We can do that for you boys. Glad you put it that way. We don't take to no one who says 'well done' here. The 'depends' part was all about the kind of meat we got and how you want it served."

She chews her gum, at least what I hoped was gum, although it's brown, and I notice a faint streak of something coating her teeth. She tosses a glance over a shoulder toward what I took to be the kitchen. "'Cause we only got red meat here. Lemme find you a table."

I begin to think that we might live after all. At least Uncle Loyal is smart enough to not press his hope for a chicken dinner with fresh greens.

We take a few slow steps behind her. I say in a loud enough voice for most of the crowd to hear, "Did I tell ya I got pulled over in Salt Lake, Pete? Yeah, the boys in blue did it to me."

Uncle Loyal finally gets into character and says, "That right, Butch? You need to be careful. They know you in Salt Lake. Am I right?" He is grinning like a five-year-old in front of the Christmas tree. He is living out a fantasy, I assume.

"Yeah. That's right. Me and blue. We don't get along so good."

We slide our way toward a small, plain wood table with two rickety chairs off in the corner of the restaurant. Uncle Loyal goes out of character again when he sees a couple of men with a dazzling array of tattoos portraying things that I had never imagined, staring at us. "Oh, excuse me. Good evening to you, gentlemen," he calls out cheerfully.

"*Stay in character!*" I hiss at him after we pass the tattoo kings, and Uncle Loyal nods absentmindedly and continues to look around the restaurant and smile and wave at people.

There isn't a menu, as such. The waitress comes by after a while and says, "Okay, you want steak, is that with a potato all trimmed out?" I do my best at growling again, "Yep, that'll be fine here for me and Pete," and she disappears again into the blue haze and dimly lighted part of the restaurant.

I say a little prayer that Uncle Loyal won't ask for salad, and if he did, it wouldn't be with the vinaigrette dressing, and if he did, he wouldn't ask for it on the side. No doubt, it would be heard in heaven and tagged "strange prayer of the day" by the ministering angels who keep track of such things. I had never prayed about salad dressing before.

"This is a most unusual place. The patronage. It surprises me. Do you think any of these people will be fishing tomorrow? They look the jolly sportsman type, eh?"

"I don't think so, Uncle Loyal," I say in a voice barely above a whisper, my eyes darting around, looking for anyone who might be wanting to eavesdrop, pull a knife, or just hit someone for the general principle of it.

"Very good, then. More open space for us. More fish for us to pursue."

To my surprise, the waitress shows up in a matter of minutes, but I guess when the meat is just a hint darker than a Santa Claus suit, it doesn't take long to cook it. She flops down a couple of big plates with the abundance of very red meat and huge potatoes and a sprig of parsley and says, "Go after it now, boys. Drinks?"

"Lemonade would be wonderful," Uncle Loyal says.

"I'll take water. No ice. Straight. No rocks," I say. "Straight water. Just water. For me. It's my ulcer. From the police messing with me so much."

"Hard drinkers, are we boys?"

"No ma'am. We just have to drive up the canyon tonight. Want to have our heads clear and our eyes sharp."

"Can't blame you for that."

"Nope. Not that."

"I'll get the water and lemonade," she says, turning toward the murky part of the restaurant/bar/biker hangout. "Lemonade. Haven't had that ordered in a year or two. Hope we got some. You, fella, you're kind of cute."

"Thank you," I say.

"Not you. I mean the little old fella."

"How kind of you," Uncle Loyal says, obviously pleased. "And you are an attractive young lady."

"Nice of you to say," she says as she saunters off. "A lotta people think so."

She comes back with the water and lemonade, and I decide to not tell her that my glass is greasy. The steak, I'd say, never really did get acquainted with the flames. Still, it tastes good. Marty was right about that. We fairly gulp down our meal, pay the bill, and I leave a big tip, because this is the kind of place where they might send out a couple of guys after you if you stiffed the waitress. We were leaving alive, after all, and for some reason, I feel that it was because the waitress thought Uncle Loyal was cute. She even winks at him as we're leaving, and to my surprise, Uncle Loyal winks back, in the way you would expect an eighty-two-year-old man to wink— deep, chaste, and exaggerated. It was with the lightness in my step of a doomed man who receives a reprieve that I walk back to the red car and head back to the cabin.

"A most satisfying meal," Uncle Loyal says. "Although I am unsure if I would return there. The people. They were quite colorful, although warmhearted and gracious."

"Another story we can tell. Aunt Barbara will never believe this one. I'll save it until we get to Utah. I want to see her face when I tell her I took you to a biker bar for dinner one night and the waitress thought you were cute. She did have some nice tattoos. Personally, I thought the cobra swallowing the puppy was charming."

"Call it this: our first fishing tale."

"Yes, our first. Only we were the bait, I think. We'll have a few more stories tomorrow."

"What time shall we start? Early I suppose."

"Yep. They usually bite best first thing in the morning. I guess fish are like us. They need breakfast too. Most important meal of the day for them and us."

I drive up the canyon toward the cabin, cozy under the trees, a happy yellow lamplight beaming into the dark night to greet us.

Fishing tomorrow. It's quiet and I am getting drowsy, and for some reason, I start to think the way I do just before I fall asleep, namely, big, random thoughts that hardly make sense.

Fish. We are fish, I think. From one water to the next, one pool to another. From creek to river to ocean, we move on, we move ahead. All of us. Uncle Loyal. Me. The people at the bar. We are fish, they are fish. We are all like fish, sometimes swimming with the current, sometimes against it, trying to figure out what's bait and what is true.

Uncle Loyal yawns, but his eyes are wide open. *He sees a lot,* I thought. He sees so much more than most people do. He called the people at the biker bar "gracious," which is a word I would not have connected with the patrons in about two thousand years of thinking. But maybe they were, in their own way. Different fish in a different current, that's all.

And driving up the canyon, on a road I'd never been on before that day, getting ready to take my ancient great-uncle on his first mountain fishing trip ever, I decide to try to find the grace in people, no matter where they were or what they looked like.

Uncle Loyal sees it. Maybe I can learn how to see it too. I'm sure it's there. I just need to look harder for it.

CHAPTER NINETEEN
WHEN YOU FISH, YOU CAST IN YOUR LINE AND NEVER KNOW WHAT YOU MIGHT PULL OUT

DARK. STILL DARK, AN HOUR or maybe more before the sun tripped over the mountains to the east. Levi rumbled in his bed, tossed and turned and, I think, might have fallen asleep again. This is an old habit from the plains. I wake up and just listen to the sounds. I wake up early. As I have aged, it becomes easier to wake up before dawn. Four or five in the morning, most days. I blink a few times and think of where I am, and then I am awake. Sometimes, I fall back asleep, but more often, I stay awake and allow myself the pleasure of slow thinking. Today, I am unsure for a few moments of where I am. The stiff bed, the air of pine, dew, and old wood walls. The cabin. Yes, the cabin we have rented in the mountains. *Today, we will fish.*

Levi bolts upright in the bed across the room. My eyes adjust to the darkness, and I see him quickly and quietly groping for his clothes and the fishing gear. We stopped at a small store on our way home from the restaurant last night and purchased more provisions for the day: crackers, juice, water, ready-made sandwiches, jerky—lots of jerky again—and fruit. Levi said, "You don't know that you're hungry when you fish because all you want to do is keep fishing, keep moving to the next hole. And then you do get hungry, and there's not enough food in the world to fill you up."

He sits on the edge of his bed for a few moments. I glance at the alarm clock. It is a few minutes after five.

"Uncle Loyal," he whispers. "You awake?"

"Yes, Levi. I'm awake. Is it time? Do we get up and get ready and go fishing now?"

"Think so. It will be daylight in an hour. I'd like to be on the creek just about the time the sun comes up."

I admit to being a little groggy, but I find my fishing clothes, laid out on a chair by Levi last night, and struggle into them. I put on a plaid flannel shirt, the pair of durable, practical cotton pants, my walking shoes, and finally, the fishing hat.

Levi nods in approval. "You look like a fisherman. That's half of it."

"I am certainly dressed for the part."

"Let's go, then. The fish await us. They tremble to know that we are on our way."

He pulls out the keys to the red car, we lock the cabin door behind us, and soon we are on our way back toward the rushing dark waters of the creek we had seen the day before. The headlights pierce the remains of the night, and we round curves in the road, moving upward, steadily climbing in elevation. Spooked, dusky deer hop across the road, one, then another, then a third and a fourth. A faint rose-and-pink light burnishes the sky eastward. Levi stares at each side road, looking at the Forest Service numbers. After thirty minutes in the car, he slows to a stop and squints at a sign.

"This is it. We turn here. This is the road Jason told us about. Fish heaven, a couple of miles away."

The road is narrow and dusty. Light reaches the tops of the trees on either side of us. A creek appears, then disappears. At a wide spot in the road, Levi pulls over.

"We need to hike . . ." and he stops and looks puzzled for a second. "We need to hike this way for no more than a quarter mile, and we'll hit the creek."

We get out of the car. Levi grabs most of our gear after handing me the two fishing poles. He looks around again, like an explorer unsure of his way. He closes his eyes and listens.

"I hear water. We'll follow this little game path until we get to the creek. We're almost there. I can smell water. I can smell pine. I can smell fish. It all adds up to the smell of victory and triumph. Beware, wily trout. You are no match for us. Levi and Loyal are at your doorstep."

I meekly follow Levi up the small trail. Soon, I also can hear the water, roiling, chattery, tumbling. Then I see it: a black ribbon, froth butting against rocks, the home of the trout, water on its merry way to a rendezvous with the sea. This moment is all so perfect. The sun splashes down in a swath through the tall trees and sends its spotlight to the clearing where we are standing. A fog or vapor rises from the stream as the sunlight touches it. Levi senses the perfectness of this moment.

"Just right," he mumbles. "Just right. Let's get you geared up."

He tosses the rubbery slick waders to me and instructs me on how to put them on. He grabs the poles and expertly ties a dry fly onto the end of my leader. He feints a cast and wiggles the pole. Then he pronounces with Biblical gravity, "We are ready. It is good."

"Which pole is mine?"

"Rod, Uncle Loyal. When you are in the mountains, they are rods, not poles. Rods for fly fishing. It is important to know the difference."

"I stand corrected."

"This one is yours."

He hands me my pole, and I try to flex it as he did. I am surprised at the play in it. It is elastic in its motion; it has a nice whip and feel to it.

"What will you wear?" I ask.

"What I have on."

"Do you want the waders? I can do without them."

"No. They're for you. With the waders on, you can get to the deeper water, the holes. That's where the fish will be in the morning. The deep holes. Where it's dark, where they have been still all night. Now they are moving with the sunlight. They'll look up and see a splotch on the water, and they'll mistake it for food. Not too bright, these fish. They can't tell the difference between a bit of steel shank and feathers and a big, meaty bug. But it's okay. If they were smarter, we would have to find a less interesting way to catch them."

"Can we share the waders?"

"No. They're yours. Now and forever. For when we fish in Utah. We *will* fish in Utah."

"Yes. I think so. I believe you. But what of you? You will be cold, your feet will freeze. This river must be like ice. You only have a pair of shorts and a T-shirt on."

"Yep. I'll be cold for a while, but then you get used to it. You never feel anything after you go numb, one of the nice things nature did for us. But I don't really notice because I'm fishing."

"You're sure?"

"I'm sure. I've done this a thousand times. Let's get to the water."

We pick our way down a small slope and stand on the edge of the stream. I can see insects hovering and skipping near the water's surface. Little wonder that fish rise and feed at this time of day. Levi motions to a spot in shallow water and says, "Go there and then cast toward the other side of the creek. Cast it just by flicking it. Let the fly drop on the water without creating a splash. You create a splash, and the fish know that someone or something is near and they will not bite. Fish are dumb, but they aren't stupid. Now wade out and try."

Wade out and try. I gingerly step into the water. It swirls around my legs, and the waders suck tight against my legs and hips. I look down for a moment and feel slightly dizzy. I am in water, I think. In the mountains with a fishing pole in my hand. A fishing *rod* in my hands.

"That's where you need to cast. Good job, Uncle Loyal. Cast over there, where it's dark."

I waggle my pole back and forth. The line gets tangled in itself, and the fly ends up pricking my left hand. I am confused. This is not how I imagined it. This is not what I thought the outcome would be. There is no magic in fishing.

"Here," Levi says.

He walks to me, sloshing through the creek. "Here," he says. And he takes my line and gently undoes the knots and loops. "Here," he says. And he stands behind me and puts his left hand on my left shoulder, and he takes my forearm in his strong right hand. "Here," he says. And with his right hand, he pulls my arm back. Gently. I feel the rhythm of his motion coursing through my shoulder, my arm, my hand, my fingers, to the whippy rod. "Here," he says. And we rock a little, back and forth, and the line splits the air, and I think I can hear a *zizzing* sound. "Here," he says, and he stops the forward motion of my hand and arm, and I watch the tiny fly float on unseen currents of air, dainty in its arc, the white speck of feathers settling on dark waters.

"Here," Levi says. And the fly lands. I wonder what a fish thinks in its watery world, if a fish can think at all, of the old man and the young man, close to one another, swaying in time with each other, while the cold water swirls about them.

"Nice, nice. That's how it should be done. Nice. Very good, very good, Uncle Loyal."

And then he says, "Here," again, and he pulls back on my arm and the line whips out of the water, with drops sparkling in the early morning sun.

And in the chilly morning waters, standing in the dizzying current, a young man, arm on my shoulder, speaking to me softly, I think of a parable.

We ride. We all ride on dark waters, bits of feather on a current. We are not strong, but strong enough. Strong enough to float, no matter how deep the water, no matter how swift it flows. *Here.* That is what He did for us. He took us in His arms and said, "Here," and there is a line that He provided. We ride the currents *here*, a slim connection of twine between us, among us. But it is a line that will not break.

I think of Daisy and my daughters. I think of my old brown house and of Carl and Harriet Van Acker. I think of John Jannuzzi, and John Fetzberg and his children on my sidewalk on snowy North Dakota mornings. I think of Glenn and the Hecht sisters. I think of Floyd McKay, and I think of slim lines and dark waters. I see their many faces on the water and think of how they are part of me. I think of strength, and it is all I can do to not simply lay my rod down in the water and turn and walk to shore and tell Levi, "I know what it is to fish now. I know."

I watch in fascination as the tiny fly bobs and floats downstream. Levi eases his grip on my arm. His left hand stays on my shoulder.

"There," he says. "There." He strengthens his grip on my right arm and helps me pull back the line and fly. I know there is something to the words he used, *here* and *there*, but I cannot think of the meaning. It doesn't come to me. "There," he repeats. "We'll do this again."

And we do. Again and again. We carefully move upstream a little, Levi holding his arm under my arm and around my back, and we try another hole, this dark place in deep water where fish stay still in the morning.

Soon, his left hand drops from my shoulder to my back and his right hand barely touches mine. Then he steps back, and our link is broken.

I am fishing on my own.

This is what Levi wanted to show me.

I know how to fish now.

The water feels cold, but the cold makes me feel alive, the way frigid air made Daisy feel alive when pellets of ice and grainy flakes of snow blew hard from the north.

Levi is never far from my side. He watches each of my movements with the care of a young father watching a child on a bicycle for the first time. Had I slipped, he would have been there, a strong hand pulling me up. I lose track of time. A vague awareness that the sun is higher in the sky and the temperature warming are all that tell me another day has taken flight, hurtling toward its sure conclusion. Levi does little fishing. A cast here and there, always with his head half cocked in my direction. I can tell he's a very good fisherman by his grace and his rhythm, the places he put his dry fly, the glowing intensity of his eyes when the fly touches water.

Then I know just enough to understand there are good fishermen and there are bad fishermen, and there are people who fish but don't care much. I also understand that the gear does not make the fisherman and you could be a good fisherman with no gear at all. I hope to be a good fisherman.

After a while and I don't know how long, an hour, maybe two, we come near a small rocky beach, and he guides me toward shore.

"Time to rest," he says. "You're wearing me out. I can't keep up with you."

"You've been good to me. I like to fish this way, wading in a stream with a light pole in my hand."

The sun feels good, shining hard on the pebbly beach where we sit. The rush of the water is musical. In the sky a hawk, maybe a red-tail, floats on the updraft from the canyon.

"But," I tell him, "I am afraid that I am not a good fisherman yet and that I am keeping you from enjoying your day."

Levi leans back, flat against the smooth stones, his feet wide apart, his arms stretched.

"Are you kidding me? You're killing me, Uncle Loyal. Any day in a place like this is a good day. Anytime you fish it's a good thing. I don't care what you fish for. It's just that you are fishing. You're *participating*. That's what counts, that's what matters. When I fish, I don't have a care in the world. I don't even care if I catch a fish, and if I catch a fish, I put it back."

I think about what he said. I liked what he said. I think again about worlds and how there are different worlds right here in front of us. I counted the worlds. There was my world, and Levi's world, the world of fishes. There was the world of the canyon and the world of the sky and the world of the sun and the world of the rocks on this beach. There was the world of the red-tailed hawk matted against the blue sky. And there was the world of the little bugs that crawled across the rocks and lived near the edge of the water. I scoop up a handful of soil.

I count all of these worlds and think of a scripture: "And worlds without number have I created." I begin to understand something that had been around me all of my life yet I've never recognized before. Worlds without numbers could mean galaxies and universes and stars and planets, and that is probably what most of us think; but it could also mean the handful of soil that I hold and the world contained therein. And for a moment, thinking these thoughts, I am happy that even a man my age can learn something new and basic and be thrilled and pleased by it all.

This bodes well, I think, of what the promise of creation and the promise of forever and the promise of worlds without numbers hold for me. So I look out at the stream and say softly, "Thank you, fish, and thank you, water. This I know now. There are more worlds than we can even begin to count."

And I think of all these things while my great-nephew Levi suns himself on this brilliant morning, alongside a stream I was fishing although I had yet to catch a fish, nor had I even had a simple bite. But in my short time fishing, I already recognized that you do not have to catch lots of fish to be a good fisherman. I hope I'm on my way to becoming a good fisherman.

A mosquito comes by and buzzes and lands on my arm, and I slap him, and his world comes to an end. Or at least it changes dramatically and rather quickly.

"Are you rested? Ready to go again?" Levi sits up and looks around. "Fish stop biting toward the middle of the day. Gets too hot, and they just go to deep water and hang out. We only have a couple more hours before they get lazy and decide they're not hungry."

"Then let us fish again," I say, and I pick up my pole and he picks up his rod, and he slips his arm around my back, and we teeter and wobble into the swift waters again.

We didn't catch any fish that morning. Not a one. Casting, I recognized, is an act of faith. Sometimes, when I laid the line out too far or it wafted behind my head into the branches of a tree, I caught a stick or a branch or a leaf, but I never caught a fish. When you go fishing, you never know what you will catch, what you will pull out. I think, "We all cast. We all cast every day. But only a few cast for fish."

Levi, I think, probably only cast about two-dozen times. Yet he is content. It is the most serene and peaceful I have seen him on the trip. *There are layers to this young man,* I thought, *and the more I peel them back, the better I like what I see.* The fast red car coming down the street of my home in North Dakota seemed as far away from me then as the North Pole. A different day. A different time. A different young man. And a different old man too.

He lets me cast into the deepest and best holes. Only once or twice is he not within an arm's length of me.

The rest of the time he is near me, keeping watch. Had I slipped, he would have been there in an instant and, no doubt, caught me or helped me break my fall. More than once, I did briefly lose my footing.

And when I did, he reached out and steadied me and always said just one word.

"Here."

And after I was straight on my feet and balanced, he always just said a second word.

"There."

Finally, I grow weary, and I say that I want to just sit on a log or a rock and rest. I tell him he can go ahead and fish upstream for a while and that I will be happy to just be still. I tell him he can have my waders because I would not need them while I sat on my rock or log.

"Are you sure? My legs are numb, and I'm used to it."

"Yes, quite sure. I will be here. When you are done fishing, just come and get me, and we will walk back to the car and then drive to the cabin."

"Well, okay. If you're sure."

"Absolutely. I hope you catch a big fish." I look around again. It is a day of incomparable beauty. I am a man of the plains, but I think, with a change of a few degrees in my life's compass, I could become a man of the mountains. I like it here. A little grassy knoll wedged between two boulders beckons me. I point it out to Levi and say, "That's where I will be. Fish as long as you like."

He says, "You're sure?"

I say, "Yes, I am. Don't worry about me. I'll be fine."

"Okay. I'll be back in about an hour. Here is my cell phone and the keys to the car, and if something should go wrong, you can always hike back to the car and call out. But I'll be back."

I see what I suppose most people would describe as a glint in his eye, one that told me that he wanted to fish fast and hard up the canyon, that there was magic for him in this canyon, and that while he had been unfailingly considerate to me as we fished, he is ready to strike out on his own and see what these Montana fish have to offer. He tugs on the waders and soon is in the river. I watch him fish the first hole, and again I'm struck by the grace and art of someone who fishes well.

I walk over to the grassy area and find a place to sit down, my legs stretched out, my head tilted back on a small stone. Though it was hard, there was a nice little crook to it, almost perfectly shaped for the head of a tired old fisherman. I cast my eyes upward again, hoping to see the red-tailed hawk. A puff of wind, this time warm, came down the canyon. Then my thoughts become slurred, my vision blurred, and I find that if I pull my fishing hat over my eyes it provides me with just the right amount of shade. I'm asleep within minutes.

I don't know how much time passed by. I rejoice in the fact that it seems we will not count time in the next life, that it is only a silly, weak man who does so now. Somehow, I hear the sloshing and trickling of water, and when I open my dreamy eyes and my thoughts have a chance to clear, I see Levi in front of me, grinning, a little like a big, wet, playful hound.

"Any luck?" I manage to say when just enough of my senses come back on the job to enable speech.

"Nope. Not a thing. I got skunked. But what a nice place and good day to get skunked."

We gather our gear and hike the mile or so back to the red car.

We follow the dirt road back toward the paved county highway. As we pull out of the canyon and back toward the cabin, I watch the small stream we had fished disappear from view. I feel as though I am bidding a friend good-bye. I will never come this way again. I know that.

Levi said he got skunked, but I have been around long enough and fished just enough to know that a North Dakota bass and a Montana trout probably smell very much the same.

Levi turns on a scratchy radio station, one that fades in and out, sings along when he knows the words, occasionally sings along even when he doesn't know the words, laughs aloud for no apparent reason more than once, and I can't help but notice how much his hands smelled like Montana trout.

CHAPTER TWENTY

LOVE CAN MAKE YOU FEEL DIZZY

I THINK UNCLE LOYAL ENJOYED fishing. He sloshed around the stream and cast his fly every which way but where it should have been, and he was so noisy that fish in the next mountain range over could have heard him coming, and they booked it for deep water. Kept me on my toes, though. The fly on the end of his rod came uncomfortably close to me more than once. One thing I didn't want to do was have Uncle Loyal perform fly-removal surgery from my ear or hand or worse. I never let him get much more than arm's length from me, and there were a couple of times he might have tumbled and taken an unscheduled bath if I hadn't reached out and caught him. I did not want to call Aunt Barbara and explain that her father had slipped, fallen, cracked a rib and a hip, and that's why she had the bill from the search-and-rescue folks that included two thousand bucks an hour for helicopter time.

But he liked fishing. I could see that. He enjoyed being in the mountains, looking at the scenery, standing in the cold water. Okay, I've got to say it, here it comes, you've been warned—I think he's hooked on mountain creek fishing.

He ran out of gas late in the morning. He told me to go ahead and fish upstream on my own. He told me he'd be fine, he just wanted to rest. It took a little convincing, but eventually I gave in. I looked at him over my shoulder before heading around a bend in the creek, and his eyes were closed, a smile on his face, and I bet he was dreaming of big fish.

Speaking of big fish, once I set out on my own, I absolutely and positively killed that creek. It was ridiculous. For a while there, about every other cast, I pulled one in. I let them all go—no reason to keep them, better to let them go back home and grow up a little—but it was one of the best fishing streams ever. Big fish, too. Most of them fourteen to sixteen inches, a couple that nudged up to eighteen. It was bliss. It was righteous. The fish would come out of the water and sort of glub at me, their little fish lips saying, "Okay, you got me. You gonna let me go or what? Please, mister? I got a wife and kids and a job finding insects . . . and, say, it's getting kind of dark out here, and I can't breathe so hot. Please?"

So in they went. I got back to Uncle Loyal early in the afternoon. He asked me if I caught anything, and I told him a bit of a lie—okay, it was a straight-up whopper—and said no, the fish just weren't biting that day. I didn't want him to feel bad. I think he believed me. I think he didn't know that my name would long be remembered by the fish in that little Montana stream: Levi, king of the creek fishermen.

We don't do much else that day, although we manage to fit in a couple of loads of laundry. We eat the leftover food that we bought the night before, except for the jerky, because I bought like twenty pounds of it, and by late afternoon, we are both back at Marty's cabin, taking a well-deserved siesta.

I wake up long before Uncle Loyal. He is sending big *Z* sounds toward the ceiling. I lay there a while, thinking about the day, the fish, the gorgeous stream and mountains. I am feeling good, feeling happy. I am also feeling lucky.

Maybe that's why I decide to sneak out of the cabin and try to dial up Rachel.

"You've got to know," Uncle Loyal told me, and he's right. I gotta know. I hike up a small rise in the late afternoon light and hope that somehow I'd get decent reception. I try to fool myself a bit, wondering if I have Rachel's phone number. Of course I do. I had it memorized. I saw it at night when I closed my eyes. I had looked at it on the scratch paper she handed me the last day of school in the spring a hundred times, loopy numbers in her thin, pretty handwriting.

"Can I get your phone number?" I had asked.

She seemed surprised. Maybe *stunned* is a better word.

"Sure, yes. Of course, Levi. Here. Wait. Let me pull a sheet of notebook paper out of my binder. Here it is. And my e-mail address. This is fine. Thanks."

"Are you sure? We've just hung out and dated once. Are you sure this is okay?"

"Yes, it's okay. I'd like it. Let's stay in touch this summer."

"Okay, we will."

I stayed in touch, sort of. I wrote her a few light e-mails that didn't say much, text-messaged her about once a week and certainly didn't tell her about my summer job. She wrote back the same kind of light, vacuous e-mails and didn't tell me much about anything other than it was really hot in Arizona, as if I didn't already know that. But I thought of her often. Correction: I thought of her all the time. I practiced what I would say to her when I talked with her. How clever I would be, how she would think, after one of my displays of brilliant conversation, "He is the man for me. I want to create worlds with him."

But I never quite could work up the courage to *call* Rachel. It's a lot easier to hide behind a text message, an e-mail, Facebook. More than once, I had the cell phone in my hand in a place free from my younger siblings, ready to talk and dazzle. But my fingers mysteriously failed to work, my brain suddenly stopped, and the only thing in my entire system that seemed to be working properly were my sweat glands and my thumping heart.

Is this love?

The room would light up. I would know that I would know. That's what Uncle Loyal said.

Could the sound of her voice light up the darkening skies of Montana?

"Only one way to find out, Levi."

Great. I was beginning to talk to myself. By the time we arrived in Utah, Uncle Loyal would have more marbles than me, and I'd be the one needing a rest home.

My heart is banging hard in my chest, my stomach, my legs, everywhere, and I have to be honest, my fingers are anything but steady when I flip open my cell phone, dial the number, and wait as the beep, beep, beep rang in my ears. An answer. A little kid. A little brother.

"Hello?"

"Hi. Is Rachel in?"

"Yeah. I'll go get her." And then I hear a shriek. "RRAACCHHEELL! It's a boy."

A few agonizing seconds go by. My heart rate goes up even more, probably pounding away at, oh, a nice steady two hundred beats per minute. My mouth goes dry. I could hang up right now and she'd never know.

And neither would I.

That's the thought that gets me. *Steady up, Levi.* I need to *know.*

"Hello?"

"Rachel! Hey, great to talk with you."

Nice, Levi. You're sounding like an elders quorum president greeting a black sheep who makes an unexpected appearance at priesthood meeting.

"Oh. Thanks."

"You'll never guess where I am. In Montana. Standing on a hill. It's almost dark, and I went fishing with my great-uncle, a guy named—ready for this—Loyal. What a crazy few days I've had."

We're not clicking. I can feel it. This is not the misty-eyed moment of magic for me. There is a void. Maybe she is engaged. Maybe the invitation is waiting for me at home. The evening air suddenly feels chilly.

"Excuse me?"

What? Here it comes. Be classy. Wish her happiness, success, health, and beautiful babies. But they could have been my babies! Our babies!

"But who is this?"

Oh no! She doesn't even know who I am. The next sound you hear is the hissing from my pretty balloon as it deflates. She's forgotten. I waited too long. She's engaged. Yes, that's it. Maybe she's married. Maybe she has a kid. No, wait. It's only been three months.

"Levi. I'm Levi. Levi Crowne. From Bountiful. Remember me?"

Of all the pathetic words ever spoken in the history of the world, and I exaggerate not, they must be *remember me* uttered in sheer desperation from a male who thinks he might be in love to the girl he thinks/hopes/fantasizes might be in love with him.

"Levi. Oh, Levi. I'm so sorry. We were eating, and it's kind of noisy here, and I guess I just didn't expect to hear from you right now."

Okay, get centered, Levi. She apologized. She didn't have to. A good sign. Take it, buddy.

"Where did you say you are?"

"Montana."

"What are you doing there?"

"It's a long story. The short version is that I flew to North Dakota, and I'm driving my great-uncle back to Utah so that he can live in a retirement home."

"That sounds very kind of you."

Kind? No. Very mercenary of me. Six hundred dollars worth of mercenary.

"He's a great guy. He's in his eighties. But he's smart and kind of funny. We're getting along great. I taught him to fish in a stream today. He seemed to like it. A lot."

"That's nice. Fishing. Wow. Fishing."

I can sense a critical juncture in the conversation. *Another one.* She does not want this conversation to veer off into the Levi Huntin' and Fishin' Manly Outdoors Show. Quick, Levi! Talk to her about something else. Save this conversation! Rise from the depths of loserville!

"How is your summer going?"

"Fine. Good, I guess. Not much to do here. What are you doing? Are you working?"

It was the question I dreaded. No internship. No clerking in a law office. No jumping out of airplanes to fight forest fires. What I am is—alright, philosophers of the world—what I am, which is what Popeye the Sailor Man used to say. At least he had his spinach. And Olyve Oyl.

"I've been working at a grocery store. It's not what I wanted to do, but the hours were good, the people were nice, and I earned enough money to get me through my senior year. I'll probably need a job on campus, too, but that's okay. I know how to work and I don't mind it."

That's it. The truth. I bagged groceries and swept the aisles. I cleaned up the messes little kids left behind. And I'd need to work my way through my senior year. My father is a portrait photographer who charges half of what he could get. That's why I need to work. Would it matter to Rachel?

If so, she didn't show it. There is a pause for a couple of seconds and something fairly amazing happens. *I stop worrying.* I don't know why, but I stop worrying and I stop trying to think of something clever to say to her. I just stop trying so hard. And the tone of our conversation changes, and the skies seem a little lighter and the air not quite as sticky.

"Do you wear a grocer's apron?"

"Yes, I do. And I look *good* in it."

"I'm sure you do look cute in it. It's probably a boring job, but if it will pay your school costs, it must be a good job."

"You're right. These days, almost any job is a good job. It meets my needs. Like they say."

"Then it doesn't matter."

I liked that answer. It *doesn't* matter.

"No, it doesn't. That sounds like something my Uncle Loyal would say. He's got a lot of wisdom. I think you'd like him."

"I'd like to meet him. Loyal. That's a name of someone who sounds wise. Loyal. It's a good name. I can't imagine anyone not understanding life with that kind of name. It just sounds that way."

I take a risk. "Someday you *will* meet him. I can work that out."

I couldn't quite believe it. *I was using Uncle Loyal to score points with a girl.* Shameless! Selfish! Trading in on one man's honor! But I didn't think he'd mind. And it seemed to work. Note to self: women dig Uncle Loyal.

"Yes, someday. I'd like to."

"It's incredibly beautiful here."

"I imagine. I've never been to Montana, but I can imagine lots of mountains and lakes, and the sky must be gorgeous."

"That's about it. There must be a million postcards of this state because everywhere you look is amazing scenery. Beautiful. Especially where we are now."

The conversation pauses, but it isn't an *awkward* pause, and I take in a deep gulp of air and listen to the chatter of birds and the air rustling the pine needles. I can almost see her smiling, eyes upward, dreaming of what the sky in Montana looks like. Come to think of it, the sky did look beautiful just then—coral and gray, pink and blue, like a big lake of colors all turned upside down.

I will take her to Montana someday, and she can see it all for herself. This is all fairly romantic, I think. I am very cool at being romantic. I have hidden skills, I am discovering.

You don't need words to make a conversation, I think. I'll need to mention that to Uncle Loyal and find out what he says. It sounds deep, like something Uncle Loyal would say. It sounds wise, at least as wise as someone my age can be. Or as wise as I can be.

"When you get back . . ." she says. Another decent sign.

"When I get back?"

"Let's get together and talk and do some things. If your uncle is in Utah, then maybe we can visit him. He might be lonely."

"I'd like that. Yeah."

"So would I." She pauses. A significant pause, I think. "Things were rushed at the end."

"They were."

"I'm glad you called."

And after that, we don't say much. Nothing much at all. Nothing that I can remember anyway, other than it all felt good and right. *She wants to see me again. I know that because she said that. Life isn't that complicated, Levi. Love isn't that complicated, Levi.*

And I remember this from Uncle Loyal, philosopher, man of light, man of wisdom, hunky heartthrob: *You will know when you know.* Do I now know? Maybe.

Somewhere when I was blasting along the plains of North Dakota, Uncle Loyal said that to me, or something very close to it. It seemed like weeks ago, maybe months ago. But what was it? Two days, three days? Not long. I can't remember. What I need to do with Rachel, what I need to do next, is figure out what kind of relationship we will have. DTR. Define the relationship. I think again of what Uncle Loyal told me. This is what he said: I need to walk into a room, a room where she is. I need her not to see me, at least at first. Then, I need her to turn toward me. And it will be then, at that moment, that second, I will see if the whole room lights up, if everyone else fades to dimness and, for me, all conversation stops and the world is set back on its heels. I will need to look at her face, look into her eyes. *And then, I need to feel if it's all right.*

My head will swim. I will feel a little dizzy. I will remember that moment forever, like when Daisy walked into the back of that small chapel, wobbling on her high heels in her homemade dress, and Loyal, just back from a war and a mission, couldn't take his eyes off her.

Yeah.

Yeah.

Yeah!

That's when I will know what I know.

CHAPTER TWENTY-ONE
I BAG A MOUNTAIN,
NO MEAN FEAT FOR A MAN MY AGE

LEVI CAME BACK TO THE cabin, and I could tell he was very happy. Was it our trek up the stream, our expedition to the high reaches of the mountains, our glorious day of trying to net the cunning trout?

I don't think so.

Our reasons for happiness often are subtle.

This is what you looked like when you went to church that first time and came home and kept repeating the name Daisy. Those were my thoughts, strong and clear as Levi threw open the door to the room and piped up, "Hello, old fishing buddy." Some moments we remember forever. I have a feeling that a conversation high in Montana's mountains is one of those moments for Levi, as mine was the first time I saw Daisy.

I believe my great-nephew has spoken to his heartthrob, the beautiful Miss Rachel. How I know she is beautiful is this: She seems to enjoy Levi's company. She seems to see him for his strengths, not his weaknesses. She seems to bring about the best in him. For these reasons, she must be a beautiful soul.

The rest of our day, at least the small sliver that was left of it, passes uneventfully. We stay in the cabin, eat leftover food from our fishing expedition, and stretch out and watch a baseball game on the cable television channel. It was, I confess, a treat for me. I have always enjoyed baseball, and since I had not bothered to get my television set repaired or replaced when it broke a few years ago, it was the first game I had seen in a long time.

We turn off the lights before ten, and I quickly drift off to sleep punctuated by sweet dreams of mountain meadow grass, tall, straight pine trees, and the sweet sound of a rushing mountain stream.

I awake at first light. Levi stirs. We pack our gear, pay the ebullient one, Marty, for our lodging, and head toward the red car.

"I talked with Marty a bit. He told me how to get over the mountains. He told me which road to take. He said it was crooked but spectacular. He said about halfway up we cross into Wyoming, and we can head straight south and get to Utah or drive west toward Yellowstone and come out in Idaho. Let's just follow our nose. Let's flip a coin, follow the sun, or play 'eeny, meeny, miny, moe' and figure out which way we'll go."

Levi had maintained his high spirits through the night. I believe him to be in love.

"Our plan of not having a plan sounds most interesting," I tell him. "We will be feathers on the wind. We will follow our hearts and follow our instincts. We will sail with a fair breeze behind us."

The day is, again, magnificent. Clear skies, a gentle wind, the promise of warmth in the afternoon chasing away the mild chill of the morning.

We quickly arrive at the junction of roads and turn to the south, driving up a high-walled canyon with yet another stream bubbling away toward the ocean. The Atlantic Ocean, I remind myself, or more properly, the Gulf of Mexico. We still had not crossed over to the west side of the Great Divide.

We journey up, always up, that first hour. Gradually, the canyon gave way to a high stone plateau. Trees become scarce as we cross above the timber line. Little lakes shimmer in the sun, pockmarking the high granite plain we twisted through. I wonder if sleek-sided rainbow trout hid in these blue waters.

I think this: *How did He think of it all? How did He plan it? Does He know each lake, pond, and stream? What does He call them in the Adamic tongue? What love He must have felt as He designed and breathed warm life to our earth.*

Levi is quiet. The scenery is unparalleled. Even he, raised in the shadow of a mountain range, is taken aback by it. Once, his voice filled with awe, he said softly, "This place. This place seems like the roof to the world."

And I agree with him. Were it night, I believe I could have reached out to one of my beloved stars, caressed it in my hand, tucked it in my pocket, and taken it away with me.

Ahead of us, we finally see the land break and give way, a gentle slope leaning toward a high mountain valley. A sign says we are at the crest, and the elevation is 10,900 feet. Before us, like a giant quilt, we see a patchwork of land: scrubby trees, the sparkling lakes, boulders as large as a house, the barren stone plains.

Without explanation, Levi pulls over at a small turnout next to a lake. Then he drives us across a rough and bumpy dirt road that leads away from the highway. We bounce and jostle down the road, which really is little more than two uneven tracks scratched across the land. We leave the small lake in the distance. Finally he stops, looks around, and I see a glimmer of a smile. We are, perhaps, a couple of miles away from the loopy mountain highway.

"We're here," he announces.

"And where is here, if I may ask?"

"Here. This is the place."

"That sounds vaguely familiar. What place?"

"Our mountain. The mountain we will climb. You'll bag your first peak here, Uncle Loyal."

He nods toward a modest ridge above the road. We are on the north side of the mountain, and a few bristly trees provide us with a bit of shade as we sit in the car. Although I am a man of the plains and claim no expertise regarding mountains, the lumpy upwelling of land seems to me very much like a hill rather than a mountain. Real mountains, I could see, are on both sides of the road, farther back, craggy and pointed. They, in late August, still have pockets of snow tucked into their shadowy parts.

"We are going to climb a mountain. Remember my promise? It was the second promise. Fish first. Climb mountain second. One down, one to go. Before we get you to . . ." and here, his voice trails off. "Before we get you to wherever, Utah, whatever, we are going to take care of this. We are going to get you on top of that mountain," he says, gesturing to the rounded ridge on the other side of the lake. "Today, we tackle this mountain, tomorrow, a new mountain, one that is taller. Next week, maybe we'll be on the top of Everest."

I ask, with caution and care, "Is that indeed a mountain, Levi?"

He scrunches up his face a bit. I can see that he is slightly annoyed with me.

"No doubt. It's a mountain, Uncle Loyal. A genuine, real mountain. I bet it's eleven thousand feet up, and that's higher than anything east of the Mississippi and a lot of places west of it. You need to remember something, Uncle Loyal. Mountains are always steeper than you think. You look at a climb and you think, piece of cake, easy, and then you find yourself on all fours, making about fifty yards an hour, holding on to a one-inch ledge for your life and hoping that your life insurance is paid up. I know. I've done it.

It's a blast. *Mountains are always steeper than you first think.* A lot of people have found that out the hard way. Hiking to the top of this one will make you break a sweat. It looks easy, but it isn't. You'll feel that. Even a little exercise, and your heart will be beating like a drum at this elevation, and I don't want to have to be the one to explain to Barbara that we lost you while climbing a mountain. Something tells me she wouldn't take that news very well."

His logic and sincerity convince me. "Let's climb my first mountain. Eh?"

"Let's."

He grabs a couple of bottles of water from the backseat. He jumps out of the car and rouses around in the trunk. Just as I am getting out of the car, he hands me my sweater, and I notice him pulling on a sweatshirt with a hood.

"For when we get to the top. We'll plan to rest up there, take a look around. At the top, the wind will be blowing, and you'll get chilled. Wrap it around your waist now, if you want to, but you'll be glad that you took it later on."

"How long will it take to climb the peak?"

He spies the hill with an expert eye. "An hour. At least. Steeper than you think. This isn't like anything you've seen back home. And I think there's a little snow pillow at the top."

So we start out. A slow, even pace, Levi in front, me behind. I must admit, he was correct about hiking at high altitudes. I become winded in the first ten minutes. Levi is most attentive, continually glancing my way, asking me how I am doing, if I am tired or short on breath. The first few times, I answer that I'm fine. Then, again I answer fine, but my head is aching and my chest heaving, and the word *fine* comes as a gasp and a puff.

"You're tougher than I am. I'm a little tired myself," he says. "Let's pull up here and sit. Couple of rocks will make a good easy chair."

It's a little game. I know it and he knows it. I appreciate his grace: pretending he's the one who's winded and worn. His ruse is to save my face and feelings. I sit down eagerly on a white rock speckled with black spots and turn to see how far we've come. I am surprised, even shocked, to see that we are perhaps a quarter mile away and a hundred feet above the small, bean-shaped lake that we had left behind. I can see the ripples across the lake, driven by a wind that we had not yet felt. The red car looks like a little boy's toy on the two faint tracks of road. I think, when we look behind, it is so often beautiful. We should look behind us more than we do.

Levi uncaps his water and swigs a long drink. My mouth is also dry, and I follow his lead. He reaches into his sweatshirt pocket and brings out a package of beef jerky.

"For energy," he says, handing it to me.

"For energy," I say and break off a piece of the salty, chewy meat and savor it. All seemed good, all seemed right at that moment. I can't not think of the strange events of my life that led me to this point. A great-nephew from nowhere, so eager and robust, so driven, and in part, so confused, who had whipped across the plains to pick me up. Someone who planned originally to drive straight through, then, I assume, collect a check, wish me luck, and whisk away again from my life and back into his.

But how was it that we came to this? Sitting near the top of a hill or ridge or mountain, the day after fishing. Looking down toward a dazzling jewel of a lake, under a milky-white sky. I realized many miles ago that Levi was changing before my eyes. And on this point of the journey, I realized another truth: I was changing as well. Because of the love that I felt for this bold, impetuous, bright, and impish great-nephew of mine, I also was learning new things. *Hidden treasures, hidden knowledge, hidden wisdom,* I thought. All here before me, all not so far from my home on the plains, but time and things to do got in my way, and I missed mountains and streams and, more so, people and family, Levi included. *If we take the time.* If we only take the time to learn about each other, to recognize the seeds of godliness and divinity in each of us. If we only stopped and saw the wonder that each human possesses. I suppose our theology implies that we were each, according to our measures, millions of years in the making, each of us a work so complex, so intricate, shaped with so much care, depth, and love. Why, then, do we not invest the time to understand each other better, to appreciate God's handiwork in each of us, at every turn in our lives? It's all there. *It's all there.* All at our fingertips.

But we are too busy, and we get distracted and our accomplishments misplaced.

At that point, I'm not too busy, sitting on my rock, in the shadow of an unnamed ridge somewhere along the Continental Divide. I feel a regret that what I was thinking, this recognition, this way of seeing life in a different and more bold way, came to me only after eight decades plus two years.

So I had learned. I felt wise for a moment, and then that went away because it had taken me so long to learn this simple lesson with the force I then felt. It may not count toward wisdom when the most obvious of life's lessons and patterns are finally recognized.

I hope that Levi had learned something from me on this journey across plains, down streams, up mountains, and into each other's lives.

The wind from the lake caught up with us; it chills me. Levi had been right about that, too. His knowledge of mountains, of high places, was unerring. My rest on the rock is complete. I feel better physically, and I will always remember this stop on my upward journey as a place where I learned something. In these few moments, I had realized a peace that felt almost indescribable. I also knew, from my eighty-two years of rambling on this earth, that the peace would be fleeting. Something would always be there to nibble at its edges or crush it with sheer, brute weight.

"We'd better get moving again," Levi says, as though he were reading my thoughts.

"Yes. You're right. Too long here and we would both be chilled. You are right. It is steeper than it looks. These high elevations can be deceiving."

"Here," he says, pulling my fisherman's hat from a pocket in his sweatshirt. "You'll be boiled like a beet up here in this thin air. Should've given this to you earlier. I didn't remember until just now. Uncle Loyal, I need to tell you this, but I think you're man enough to take it. You don't have much hair. No protection. I hope this does not come as a surprise to you, but you are bald, and you need your hat."

"Well, not only a surprise, but it comes also as an offense. I didn't know I was bald. I thought I had a full head of hair and was an extraordinarily handsome man."

"You are, Uncle Loyal. You are proof that a man doesn't need hair to be handsome. Think of all the men who shave their heads these days. You were just ahead of your time. And natural about the way you did it. Now put on the hat."

"Well, if you say."

"I say. Let's get moving again."

"We have a mountain to climb. Eh?"

He laughs lightly. "Yeah. Correct."

We start upward again. Levi finds a sturdy, dead tree limb for me to use as a staff. It makes the climb much easier. We rest several times more. He was absolutely right about how I would react in the thin mountain air. Near the end of the hike, I gasp, swigging for air the way a parched man seeks liquid. Perspiration trickles down my forehead and the back of my neck. I drank most of my water. I can feel the stiffness seeping in of muscles not used in this way for many years.

And each time we rest, I look back and see something new.

Above us, the sky grows from sharp-blue to pearl-blue then milky-white as high clouds creep in.

Finally, we make it to the top of the hill or ridge. But to me, by then, it had become a mountain. I am grateful that Levi had chosen wisely. Had we tried for a higher peak, I would not have made it to the top. I now know that you must choose with care which mountains to climb.

A little patch of snow is just over the ridge top, sheltered from the sun. I take off my shoes and socks and step into the snow. I wiggle my toes and smile. I had climbed my mountain and felt the snow on my feet. Goal achieved. Levi pulls out his little phone and snaps a photo of me. Proof that I, Loyal Wing, climbed a mountain, well into my eighties.

"For posterity," Levi announces.

"Yes, for posterity."

"And to freak out Barbara."

"Yes. To freak out my daughter."

We sit and rest, wordless for a few minutes.

Silently, Levi takes my staff from me and pushes it into the ground. He gathers pebbles and rocks, and only after a few minutes could I see that he'd arranged them to form my name.

"It's your mountain now, Uncle Loyal. You bagged it. That's what you say when you get to the top of a mountain. You bagged it. Not bad for a guy your age. Not bad for a guy thirty years younger than you. You are," he pauses for dramatic effect, "a beast."

"I have never been called a beast before. I think I like the sound of it."

A wind, more cutting and blustery than what we had experienced to that point, rumbles up the ridgeline. I notice that the sky has lost its luster and that a squall line is moving toward us at a great rate of speed. We are going to get wet. And in this wind, we are also going to get cold.

In the distance, and it was impossible to tell if it came from above or below, we hear the low, throaty growl of thunder.

"We'd better head down. Get back to the car before we get really wet. These storms can sneak up on you. It shouldn't take us long," Levi says with what I took to be a hint of worry.

We hurriedly make our way off the mountain, although I wished we could have stayed longer. The dark clouds maw behind us, and once, when I looked back, the clouds indeed had split into two fingers, looking much like jaws ready to gobble us up. Lightning splays down into the lake-side basin before us. Levi keeps an anxious eye on the sky and where the lightning touched down. The thunder explodes, as loud as any I had heard at my prairie home. With no more than a quarter mile to the car, the plopping drops of rain change into a torrent as we half hop, half jog our way over the rock-strewn field. I stumble once or twice; my legs and knees and arms seem to betray me as I awkwardly crab my way down the hill. Finally, we reach the car. Levi quickly unlocks the passenger door and gently shoves me in. Outside I watch with awe my first, and to this point, only Montana gully-washer.

We are soaked, we are tired, we are cold. And we are happy.

Levi starts the engine and turns up the heat. He begins to crawl the car down the hillside, back toward the main road, making sluggish progress measured in yards by the minutes. Near the bottom of a small ravine, he pushes hard on the accelerator toward a shallow puddle of water that had been given birth by the storm.

The car lurches forward then stops. Levi pushes hard on the accelerator. Nothing happens. I hear the *zizz* of the front wheels turning, cawing their displeasure. Lightning spikes down around us. Rain pounds the car. Levi flips the gear shift from forward to reverse, forward to reverse, forward to reverse, trying to rock us out of the puddle, which, even in the short time we were there, had become more like a pond.

Finally, he puts the car into park and lets the tired engine pant. His eyes are focused straight ahead, his jaw tensed. The warm air blows out of the heater vents. The windshield swipes move rhythmically.

We are two sailors in a boat stalled on a sea by a wheezy and temperamental storm. For the second time in four days, the fury of nature has crossed us.

Water dripped down the side of the car windows. It had grown unnaturally dark as the big storm swirls above us and around us. Quite suddenly, it seemed as though nightfall had overtaken us with the suddenness of a stealthy bandit.

Levi looks straight ahead. His mouth curled almost to a downward, perfect semicircle.

"Uncle Loyal," he says deliberately. "We have a problem. We're stuck."

CHAPTER TWENTY-TWO
SITTING IN THE RED CAR,
MY LIFE TURNS TO GUMBO

DUMB. VERY DUMB. HOW COULD I have let this happen? A perfectly awesome day. We start early, get to the top of the mountain, and then, boom! The day goes down the tubes. Disaster. We're stuck, very far from anywhere. People die doing stupid things like this. What did John Wayne say in a movie? Life is tough. It's even tougher when you're stupid.

I saw the storm coming. I knew what it could mean. I've been in the High Uintas when a storm like that comes blasting in. You don't take your time, you don't goof off, you get right down to business and find someplace safe. I've read about too many people who are sunning themselves one moment at the top of a mountain, ignore a few clouds, and all of a sudden they're crispy critters.

So there we were. Stuck in the gumbo. Here is the recipe for Montana gumbo: drive off a paved road, add a barrel of water to the dirt, whip it up with wind, and let it thicken. And harden. Like cement. There is no escape.

I did not want to spend the evening in the middle of the mountains, but it was late afternoon and the possibility of calling the car home for the night was growing larger by the minute as the puddle around us grew and the thunderstorm showed no sign of quitting.

What do I do? Apologize. Why do I always apologize for everything?

"I'm sorry Uncle Loyal. I should have seen it coming. (I did.) We should have hustled out of here sooner. (True.) I shouldn't have tried to splash through the puddle. (Also true.) I should have got out and seen how deep it was and how slick. (Hindsight is always 20/20.)"

"Well, stuck we are and stuck we shall be until it dries out or someone rescues us or until we find a way out of this predicament," Uncle Loyal said in a most pleasant tone of voice. "It's fine, Levi. There is no need to apologize."

He is so calm. Steady. A rock. Unflappable. It's funny, but just hearing him made me feel a little better. Zen Mormon, that was Uncle Loyal.

I begin to think, which only came about thirty minutes too late. Maybe I could get us unstuck. *Brain, click in. Brain cells, line up and get back to work. Let's see.*

"This is what we're going to do, Uncle Loyal. I'm going to get out and find a bunch of rocks and wedge them under our back tires to get us a little traction. That's what we need. Traction. Traction is good."

He looks at me with his eyebrows arched into a high triangle on his forehead.

"Eh? Are you certain, Levi? Back wheels or front? Why not at least wait until the rain slows and try something then?"

"Can't wait. I want to try it now. Back wheels, definitely. We're losing time. And daylight. This puddle is only going to get bigger. A puddle I can deal with. Getting us out of a pond, now that's another thing. And we're going to be stuck in a pond if this rain keeps up."

"As you wish."

With nothing less than a sense of doom, I climb out of the car. My foot instantly sinks into about a foot of water, disappearing in the brown foam with an ominous sucking sound. I turn my head and smile at Uncle Loyal, a smile purely for show.

"It's not so bad, not as bad as I thought," I call, a smile made of pure, 100 percent synthetic products plastered across my face.

Confidence, man, I say to myself. *You're the captain of this car or ship or whatever it really is, and you have to be confident or the passenger might start to panic,* although it was difficult for me to imagine Uncle Loyal panicking over anything.

"It appears your foot is stuck in mud," Uncle Loyal leans over and says, a frown creasing his face.

"Yes. It appears my foot is stuck in mud." I try to not sound as though I were making fun of him, but I probably didn't succeed. A profound grasp of the obvious, has this great-uncle of mine.

There was only one thing to do next and that was swing my other foot into the muck. Laugh in the face of danger. Embrace trouble. Fear nothing. Stick your good foot into the muck. My other foot nestled with the same sucking sound into the mud.

At this juncture in my life, I am able to predict with certainty several things.

One, I am going to get muddy.

Two, I am going to get wet.

Three, my plan has zero chance of working.

Four, we are going to spend the night in the mud puddle.

Other than those four trifling details, everything is fine, just fine. Fine. Yes. Fine.

But I have to push on. With slow, exaggerated steps, I make my way across the puddle, which is now close to twenty yards wide. I begin to find rocks and take off my sweatshirt, which then doubled as a wheelbarrow, although it had no wheels and couldn't carry much. Other than that, it worked really well. I sling my sweatshirt over my shoulder and trudge back into the puddle/pond/lake and, with much more confidence than I feel, dump the load behind one of the rear tires. I repeat this process about a half-dozen times as Uncle Loyal looks on with a mixture of curiosity and bemusement. At the end of the last load, soaked, cold, and filthy, I reach down and try to push the rocks against the tires. I force a smile and give Uncle Loyal what must have been the most hypocritical thumbs-up signal in the history of all humankind.

The moment was now at hand.

I try, with very limited success, to clean myself up before hopping back in the car. I did have the foresight to ask Uncle Loyal to toss a couple plastic grocery bags on the seat to protect it from the slimy swamp creature who was about to get in and try to drive the car out of our misery.

"You are wet," Uncle Loyal says as I gingerly climb in. "And dirty."

I let out a long sigh. Wet, yes. Muddy, yes. Stupid, that too. The shadows are lengthening, and so is my shame. I'd seen the storm coming. I couldn't get around that. I'd seen it coming and knew it could mean trouble, and still I did nothing, or at least I didn't do anything quickly enough to avoid getting us in this jam.

I might have avoided all this if I had only not driven full blast into the puddle but instead gone around the edges of it. But no, I was in a hurry and maybe feeling a bit like the hero, and I was driving a hot red car, and I headed for trouble with my eyes wide open and the part of my brain that usually flashed the caution sign totally shut down.

There was a great sacrament meeting talk in here somewhere, but I am too frustrated and embarrassed to dig it out. I have other things to dig out first: Loyal. Me. The car.

I start the car and gently step on the accelerator. We might have moved an inch or two, then we settle right back in. I try again. Then again. And again. We made no progress.

"Let me get out of the car and push. You can slide over, Uncle Loyal, and step on the gas pedal while I'm pushing in the back. Maybe that extra shove will get us going. If the car does start to move, just keep going until you get out of the puddle. I'll catch up with you."

"You'll get muddy," Uncle Loyal warns, giving me a long, sad glance. "But I guess you already are."

I swing the door open and step into the ooze again. I muck my way around to the back of the car as Uncle Loyal moves to his left and grasps the steering wheel. With more hope than I feel, I shout, "Now!" and begin to push on the back of the red car, which now was more the color of a baked potato. With all my might, I push. The car wheels spun; I lose my footing and do an Olympic-caliber face-plant in the mud. In my mind, I see a row of judges all holding up cards that read "10."

This is not going to work, I think.

Uncle Loyal stops the engine and looks behind the car. He rolls down the window and gazes at me wordlessly for several seconds. I am coated in mud and must look like the creature from the swamp. I had to wipe away the area around my eyes just so that I could open them. I am grateful that Rachel cannot see me at this moment.

At last, Uncle Loyal speaks. I think, what he's going to say would be calming and profound and would help us to find a way out of this predicament. *Listen, Levi. Listen well. The voice of wisdom is about to thunder down to you from the top of the mountain.*

"You're muddy, Levi. Quite muddy."

"Great. This is just great," I mumble. Then I sit down right in the middle of the puddle-turned-pond, figuring I couldn't get any wetter and couldn't get any dirtier. It is at this point that I remember I have a pair of almost-new waders in the car trunk. Terrific, Levi. Smart, Levi. Way to think it all through, pal.

And there, at that moment, I feel so utterly lost and alone.

It's evening, I'm stuck in the mountains of Montana, I am muddy and tired and frustrated, and it is still raining. Less than twenty-four hours ago, I'd felt on top of the world after talking with Rachel, nothing could go wrong, that life was filled with promise, that I had my course clearly in front of me. And now I feel I am sitting below the world. I am in a huge mud puddle, hopeless and helpless. My life had turned into a muddy Montana gumbo.

Uncle Loyal calls out to me, "I have a towel, Levi. I'll hand it to you through the window. And I'll fetch you some dry clothes. It is a very good thing we did some laundry yesterday. Let's start there, with a towel to get you cleaned up, and we'll proceed forward, eh?"

Let's start there. Okay, he's right. When you're sitting in a puddle, cold and wet, you have to turn it around. I had to start somewhere. Why not with a towel and some dry clothes? Take a small victory, I think. When you're sitting in a mud puddle with no way out, take a small victory.

I towel off and slosh around to the back of the car. With great care, I change my clothes and feel a tiny bit more like a member of the human race.

I'd seen it coming. I'd seen those clouds. I'd known it could mean trouble. Why didn't I act or react or do something?

I still can't answer.

"It's okay, Levi. All is well. We're dry, we have shelter, we have food. Jerky. We have lots of jerky. And think of the story we'll be able to tell Barbara and your family when we get back. Men alone, lost in the foreboding Montana mountains, fighting against the beastly elements."

"We might be here all night."

"We might. And that's fine too. All is well."

I think of my cell phone. I doubt, considering that I was in the middle of a wilderness and my closest neighbors likely were bears, mountain goats, wild chickens, vultures, and elk, that I would be able to get in touch with anyone up here. I had actually thought of trying to call someone when we first got stuck, but there were two problems with that idea: one, I am a male and don't like to ask for help, especially from strangers, and two, I am a male and don't like to ask for help, especially from strangers.

But now it's worth a try. Thankfully, I had the sense to take my cell phone out of my pocket before I decided to take a swim in Mud Lake. I reach into my backpack, where I had set it, flip it open, and see the low battery sign flicker once before the phone shuts down. I had forgotten to charge it after my call last night. I was out of juice and out of luck.

"We're stuck," I report. Again.

"Yes. I know that."

"Well. Here we are."

"Yes. Here we are."

"Tomorrow. Tomorrow morning, if the weather is good, I'll hike down to the road and flag someone down, and we'll get some help. But I can't think of anything to do right now."

"Nor can I. We have a plan, Levi. Always good to have a plan."

Outside, the rain has slowed to a patter. Off to the west, the sky is lighter, and I can even see a few yellow rays of sun peeping through the jumbo gray clouds. The storm is almost over. I know that the chances of having a good day tomorrow are in our favor. Summer storms come and go quickly. That only leaves the problem of how to spend the night.

"One of us can sit up front, and I suppose the other one can curl up in the back. We have extra clothes, so we'd better layer up," I suggest. "Gonna get cold up here tonight, summer or not."

"I'll just lean the seat back and spend the night here," Uncle Loyal says. "You can take the backseat. You can stretch out some there. I have a few extra clothes in my suitcase. A sweater or two, a jacket. If you can get to the trunk, we can put on the extra clothing. It might be well-advised. I have a suspicion that you are right; it will be cold up here, even in August."

Extra clothes was an offer I can not afford to pass. I take off my dry socks before going back out into the rain and slowly making my way to the back of the car, where I pop the trunk lid and rummage through Uncle Loyal's large suitcase. I find the clothing he mentioned then slosh and slide my way back into the car. There isn't any need for the waders because I'm already covered in mud. Once again, I'm feeling cold and muddy and mad at myself for getting us into this mess.

I check my watch. That old familiar gray light of evenings in the mountains is overtaking us. It is a little after eight. It would be pitch black in twenty minutes, and stone quiet, too.

To my surprise, I begin to feel drowsy. I climb into the backseat and stretch, as best I could, across it. Not a four-star lodge, but for a night, it might do. "I'll leave the keys in the ignition, and the heat on high. When it gets cold, one of us can reach over, start the car, and let the heater blast on us for a few minutes. At least we won't freeze to death. And we shouldn't starve, either. We've got a ton of food. Heat. Food. Water. We have a lakeful of that. So we're okay. More than okay. Maybe I'll fish that little lake in the morning. From the car window."

"You are very resourceful, Levi."

"Promise me this, Uncle Loyal. I get to tell this story, not you. And you can't mention a word about it to Rachel unless I give you the wink and nod. Promise. My eternal well-being might be in your hands. Little Levi babies are depending on you. We don't want Rachel to know until after the wedding that she is marrying a klutz. Let's just say it's our little secret."

"You have my solemn promise, Levi. You sound confident of your choice and chances."

"But I'm not."

"And why do you think that is? If I may ask."

"You may ask. We've been through a lot together, Uncle Loyal. No secrets, eh? We both fell in love with Evelyn. Or was it Vicky? Something with a *v* in it. We survived the biker bar together. We went fishing. We climbed a mountain. We got caught in a roaring, rain-swollen torrent and swam to safety. We rescued a van load of Girl Scouts from the raging flood. We changed the tire for a bus filled with nuns on a field trip to the mountains. We fought grizzlies with our bare hands. We sunk a pirate ship in a battle on the lake. We did all of these things, or something close to them. All that. So, yes, you can ask why I am not feeling confident."

"Very well, then. Why?"

"It's like this . . ."

And then I couldn't think of a thing. *Not a thing.* Other than I am muddy, tired, and lying down in the backseat of a rental car wondering when we'd get out of this nightmare. "Last night I felt on top of the world after talking with Rachel. Now I feel like the whole world has landed on me."

"Understandable. We are very harsh on ourselves," Uncle Loyal says. "You especially seem to have that tendency. You set high expectations for yourself. Look at it this way. Into every life a little rain must fall. We happened to have more than just a little today, eh? We had a flash flood, something I've experienced a time or two in North Dakota. I think what you're feeling is normal and to be expected."

His voice, as usual, was soft, calm, and comforting. I think if a nuclear bomb ever went off, Uncle Loyal would look at the mushroom cloud and say, "My. That was a loud explosion. Now. See. Look at that cloud forming. How interesting."

I think for a while, maybe five minutes. Levi having quality time with Levi. The gears of my mind engaged. Uncle Loyal seemed to sense (Doesn't he seem to sense everything?) that I am in deep thought, at least by my standards, and was waiting for me to speak. Finally, I come up with just the right thing to say, something that describes my feelings, my outlook on life, my psychological and emotional profile at that instant. I reach way down, way back. This was important. I clear my throat. I want Uncle Loyal to hear what I am about to say.

"You see, Uncle Loyal, I have *issues*."

"Oh. Issues?"

"Yeah. Issues. You know, issues."

"Oh."

"Oh?"

"Yes, I said 'oh.' I'm not entirely sure what you mean by issues."

"Issues. They are, well, you know. Problems, I guess. But not quite problems. They're issues. Problems with a mental twist to them."

Bet that explanation cleared it right up for him.

"I see. Or at least I believe that I see," Uncle Loyal said. "And what might these issues be?"

"I don't know. Yeah. Wait. I do. How I feel about things."

"What things?"

"Everything. Life. Love. Career. What I want to be when I grow up. My struggle with trying to be mature. Those kinds of things. Nothing big. Just those things. Trivial matters."

I sit up in the back of the car. The sun, in its last-ditch effort of the day, once again breaks through the gray clouds far to the west, scattering rays of light on the tops of the ridges and partway down to the lake. For a moment, the rock bowl we are stuck in takes on a rosy color and the waters of the small lake appears crimson and gold. The few trees on the other side of the lake take on a dark, dusky shade of green. It is a beautiful sight, and I have a crazy thought: the view at that moment was almost worth the whole misadventure of getting stuck miles from nowhere.

"Tell me more about Rachel," Uncle Loyal suggests.

"I can't. It's funny. The truth is I don't know that much more about her. It's all a feeling and, I guess, an attraction at this time. She wants to teach elementary school. I know that. She's from Arizona, where I served my mission, but we met back at school."

"A school teacher. A noble profession," Uncle Loyal says slowly. "Something that Daisy once considered. Tell me this, if you can. How do you feel when you are around her?"

I think a bit on this. He said "around" her, not "about" her. If he said "about," that would be easy—she's pretty, not big, not small, I like her a lot, she's fun, she has dimples. But that's not *really* what he asked. I think about what I might say, what could come tumbling out of my mouth, that I felt happy, smart, handsome, worthwhile, or any other number of adjectives when I was around her. I think about it, and then I say something that surprises even me.

"I like myself when I'm around her. I feel all right about things. I feel good. I feel content. That makes no sense, does it?"

Uncle Loyal turns around and looks directly at me. In the dim light, I can barely make out his features—the high, smooth forehead, the arched eyebrows, the folds of skin hanging limp from his chin. But I can see something in his eyes, something that tells me my answer made a good impression on him. I've read and heard about eyes that sparkled my whole life, and it never made much sense to me. I always figured it was a writer's trick because eyes don't sparkle; they can't, there's no electricity hooked up. Or so I believed. But here I am, at dusk, stuck in the mountains in a fairly dark car, about to spend my night in the backseat shivering, and I can see his eyes, and his eyes are definitely sparkling, little flashes that catch the last of the day's light.

"A very fine answer, indeed. I always liked myself when I was around Daisy. She brought out the best in me. Little else matters when one is considering matrimony. If you are content and she is content and you bring out the best in each other, then all will be well with you, my young nephew."

Content? That's not what the world would have you believe. I need an appointment with Dr. Phil to talk about this one.

I had never really thought about being just content around Rachel all the times we hung out. It seemed as though I always had to prove myself around the girls I dated. I had to be and wanted to be *more*. I wanted them to have *more*. I wanted to promise them *more*. And look at what it had accomplished so far. No missus in my life, no diamond ring on her hand, no gold ring on mine, no little sons and daughters of the tribe of Levi to spice things up. I wanted *more*, but all I had was *nothing*.

Is there a message here for me?

All of the people I knew my age, they all seemed to have *prospects*, while I didn't. They all seemed to be on their way to *more*, but I wasn't. They all seemed to be on the up escalator for a very long ride, express ticket to the top, while my way up was more a rickety ladder with not many rungs. They knew things I did not. And what I have accomplished, the good things I had going for me, it almost seemed as if I *begged* to get them. Even my paltry, humbling job as a grocery store bagger came only as a result of intensely begging the store manager to hire me.

Uncle Loyal, from the gathering dusk, asks me a question, a question that startles me a little. "What does your father do for a living?" We were talking about me and my issues, and then he asks me something off the track. Or so I thought.

"He's a photographer. He takes family portraits. You can't believe how many families have one of his shots hanging above their mantels back home. Thousands. I mean, literally thousands. He's really good at what he does"—and here I pause, and I think, *Yes, he* is *good at what he does*. He's a fine photographic technician, he works hard, he treats everyone fairly, and he puts genuine feeling into each photo he takes. He is a perfectionist about his photos, not for his own sake, but because he wants his customers to be happy with what he provides them. Just about then, the little guilt buzzer went off about Dad after about a dozen years of relative silence. Okay, I admit it. When the conversation came around to "What does your daddy do?" I tended to gloss over it, and I had since a long time ago, way back to junior high when my dad came to take our class photos. For some reason (and here I pause to insert a note to myself—*it was pride, Levi, just plain pride, deal with it.*) I tried to get in and out of conversations about him as fast as I could. My dad is not a doctor, lawyer, engineer, dentist, accountant, businessman—heck, he's a lousy businessman, we all know that—and it seemed a little embarrassing to say, when asked what he did for a living, "He's a portrait photographer."

Uncle Loyal turns around in the front seat and seems to be looking at the dark black hole just to the left of us, the now-still lake bed.

"Ah. What a beautiful and honorable profession. What a wonderful thing to do with one's life. To make people happy. To freeze them in a moment of time when they were joyful, when they looked their best, when they were together. That we all could be photographers. Your father, I imagine, is a good and gifted man."

I don't say anything. At least at first. Uncle Loyal's words were pounding like big ocean waves into my skinny little soul. For some reason, tears well up in my eyes, and all of those times when I was reluctant to talk about what my father did for a living seemed to burn a hole right through me. I'm thankful it's dark so that Loyal couldn't see me. I'd never heard my father complain about his job, what he earned, the occasional families who were rude to him or who stiffed him on their bills, and I'm sure he had more than a few of those through the years.

My dad was just a nice guy who was good at what he chose to do.

This was starting to sing to me. I didn't need to beg. I didn't need to ask for forgiveness or approval for who I am, who my father is, the way we are. It is time to say something to Uncle Loyal, who seems to be staring into the heavens, looking for the first great evening stars. Loyal and his stars. He had to be looking for his stars. He is a man who, given the choice of looking into the heavens or looking into the mud, would always cast his vision upward.

So I answer. My voice is croaky, and I feel like a thirteen-year-old again, when the first major change of life came. I hope Uncle Loyal chalks it up to the rapidly cooling night air. "Yes. You're right, Uncle Loyal. He makes people happy. We never went without anything we needed. He is a good and gifted man. I'm proud that I am his son. And my mom is a lot like him too. I have good parents. The best."

"Your father need not be a mystery to you, Levi. He must be a content man. A happy man. A peaceful man."

"I think he is."

"It's a gift, a skill, the ability to be content. But I am unsure if you are born with it or if it is learned. No. I believe you must learn how," Uncle Loyal says. "Part of acquiring wisdom, I suspect. There must be a chapter in the book of wisdom about being content."

"Yeah. You've got a point."

How could I have missed it? My parents were right there, always, good people, living a simple, good life, devoted to family, but I didn't recognize the beauty in who they were and what they did. How could I have missed it? But I did. I had. Until now. Stuck in the mud in Montana.

And then it seems as though Uncle Loyal peels the skin right off my skull, looks into my brain, my mind, maybe even my heart. He looks inside and *sees* what I am thinking. He looks at me and knows. *He knows.* I am convinced it is not just a lucky guess. He knows.

"I have yet to know anyone who wanted more and was content, who wanted more and was at peace with himself. It's such a simple thing. But it's a small bit of knowledge that not many people truly understand and fewer yet embrace."

Note to Levi: Significant moment here. What's he saying? What's the meaning? The gears in my head are grinding away. It is this: *Levi, you can't always be on the hunt for more things, more stuff, more to do, more power, more authority, more of . . . more of whatever, and be at peace with yourself. It does not compute. It defies spiritual physics. It's oil and water, Levi. It's opera and bad heavy metal. It's home cooking and Scout camp food. It's lima beans and apple pie a la mode.*

Do the math: it does not add up.

I roll over on my right shoulder. I think, *I could take up the camera. I could follow in my father's footsteps. Maybe that is the path for me. I don't know.*

"This sounds paradoxical, Levi. But I have given thought to it for many years. In this old life, you actually gain more by not wanting more. I hope that makes sense."

I just say, "It does."

Uncle Loyal leans back in his chair. I look out the car window and see the stars, brilliant stars, puncturing the blackness of the summer sky. The storm is over. Tomorrow it would be clear and warm, the sky, that brilliant blue you can see only at high elevations. With daylight, I'd be able to figure a way out of the mud puddle we are trapped in. It was an odd sensation that night, knowing we are surrounded by water, far from anyone or anywhere, no solid plan to get us out. But with Loyal in the front seat, a half tank of gas, and enough chips and jerky to feed us for a week, I stop worrying. *There is a way out.* We'd find it, and we'd laugh about our night in the muddy red car for years to come. I decide to show myself the same forgiveness that I would bestow on others. What a concept!

We don't talk anymore. Uncle Loyal's words about gaining more by wanting less settle comfortably into my thoughts. I feel peaceful, more than I had in a long time. I begin to think of all the territory we'd covered in just a couple of short days, what we'd seen, and more important, what I had learned. I was understanding the road and what I could learn about life from the people I came across on my travels. I was beginning to recognize how a trip was changing into a journey for me. With Uncle Loyal sitting next to me in the front seat, this trip from North Dakota to Utah was certainly becoming a journey.

The little slip of the moon rose over the lake. There was no sound. It was still, still.

I fall asleep more easily than I had imagined possible. A few times during the night, I hear Uncle Loyal turn on the car engine and feel the blast of warm air flowing into the backseat, where I lay curled and, to my surprise, content.

When the morning comes, red and dazzling, I am amazed at how much of the puddle around us has disappeared.

CHAPTER TWENTY-THREE

WE ESCAPE THE MOUNTAINS AND ROLL WITH UNCERTAINTY TOWARD OUR DESTINY

QUITE THE TALK I HAD with my great-nephew. I hope I did not discourage him. Nor do I hope he took what I said too seriously.

Levi is an unusual young man. He struggles within himself, but in time, he will figure that out. His sense of humor is alive and crackling; he makes me laugh, which is good for me. I have not laughed often enough these last few years. He shows great promise. He understands life fairly well for someone of his tender years. In him, I see hope; I see the future. I see someone who is not willing to take life in any one particular way because it is expected of him. Obedient, yes. Independent thinker, also yes. The two are not incompatible. Levi could be a plainsman.

He has the capacity to be wise.

I did not sleep well. The setting was beautiful as the night draped itself over our little carved bowl in the mountains. The air was strong with scent of the water, I suppose, from the small lake, the spiky aroma of the alpine country. At least it seems like it is alpine country. I am a flatlander and not acquainted with the nomenclature of these high spires of granite. Each time I would think of it—*Loyal, you are in the mountains at a high elevation, marooned in a dashing red car with bears on the prowl and the chance to tell tall tales when liberated*—I would get excited and find slumber difficult to achieve.

It was also cold. The cold of the mountains nips at your edges, darts from your head to your feet. It settles upon you in subtle ways—a chill in the shoulder, a stinging at the toes, a shudder down the bumpy spine. Unlike the cold of the plains, it is where the temperature and wind drive through you like a blue, chilled, steel stake.

Midnight gradually turned to morning. I was happy to see the first gray light of dawn. Levi was still asleep and seemed peaceful. I began to think of ways that we might extricate ourselves from this woeful predicament.

I did not need to apply much thought to it. Soon after daybreak, when the shadows were still long and the first hope of warmth was manifesting itself, I hear the sound of an engine grinding slowly up the mountainside. In a quarter hour, I can see the headlights from a truck, a green-painted fire engine of some kind, patrol lights mounted on its cab.

Levi sits up suddenly. He rubs his eyes and runs his fingers through his hair. He cranes his neck and starts to say something, but his words come out as an early-morning slur. His breath is warm and sour, his movements jerky. Then he also hears the engine.

"Forest Service or BLM rig," he says. "Probably out on fire patrol. All that water from the storm, and they're looking for fires."

"Will they stop for us?"

"Oh yeah. Out here in the woods, you always stop for everyone, especially if they look like they could use a hand. It's just the way it's done." He pushes his hands against his face, looks around, and seems to take stock of our surroundings. "And I think we could use a hand. Call me crazy. But I think we're still stuck. That much didn't change during the night."

We watch with hopeful anticipation as the truck crawls up the mountain, sometimes disappearing from sight, the noise from its engine fading. I remind myself that this is natural and normal, the flow and ebb of sight and sound at high elevations. Certainly they would not turn away.

I am on the verge of blowing the car horn or asking Levi to take to his feet and dash down the mountain to flag the attention of the crawling engine's crew. Then, almost as if by miracle, the big truck lumbers its way into view, not more than one hundred yards from us. It is a moment of pleasure, of celebration. They had seen us. Our rescue is at hand. I swing open the door and crane my head out and wave an arm in the crisp air.

The engine pulls up to the edge of our wide, muddy puddle. Two young men and a young woman dressed in bright yellow shirts and sturdy green pants hop out.

"Good morning," the tallest of the three calls out. "Looks like you're in a fix. Mind if we help you out?"

"Not at all. We would be obliged. We got caught in a thunderstorm. It was a calamitous event. Before we knew it, we were in the middle of this pond. My great-nephew heroically tried to free us, but he said the mud was ferocious and unforgiving."

"That it can be," the tall one says, knowingly, affably. "You're not the first people we've pulled out of a jam like this. We're supposed to be looking for new fires, but after a gully-washer like last night, we're more likely to find people stranded in mud or water."

One of his companions, a short, stout fellow with long red hair and sprigs of a fuzzy red beard, comes to his side. "You took the last one. Sarah the one before. My turn, I guess," he says with uncommon good nature. "I don't suppose either of you will want to go play in the mud this early in the day."

"All yours, Nate."

And with that, he pulls a cable on a winch at the front of the truck, and in mere seconds, had sloshed his way to the car and hooked us to the engine. The young woman flips a switch and, with no apparent effort, the line goes taut. With a smucking and swooshing sound, Levi's red car is pulled to dry land.

"Thank you. Thanks so much. Cool. Thanks. Awesome," Levi speaks in rapid-fire fashion, getting out of the car. "We had a plan and we were just ready to get on with it, but you guys saved us the trouble. Did I mention I spent a lot of time in the mountains? In Utah. I know my way around stuff like this. But you guys made it look easy."

"Don't be so sure of that," the young woman says dryly. "You're in the Beartooth Mountains, and a half-dozen people a year who don't quite know what they're doing walk or drive in here and never come out. It's rugged back here. Steep as a goat's face, dark as a cow's stomach. They get turned around and panic. Can't even remember to walk downslope. Gone. Disappeared. Dead and never seen again." Here she pauses for dramatic effect. "Bear bait."

"It was Sarah here you need to thank," the red-bearded one says. "Way down on the highway, she thought she saw a glint in the sun. We figured it could be trouble for someone, so we decided to take a look. Part of what we get paid for is side trips like this."

Levi looks embarrassed. I know he wants to do something, say something that indicates he's no greenhorn lost in the mountains, but it was no time to put forth that he is an experienced mountaineer and almost an Eagle Scout. There is nothing he can do but nod and mumble, "I guess so. Thanks, again."

I try to push a twenty-dollar bill into the hands of the tall one, but he shakes his head. "Just doing my job. Good luck to you. We'll follow you back down to the state highway. In case you have any other problems, we'll be right behind you."

Levi gets into the car, still smarting from the young woman's mild rebuke. He starts the engine, and away we go, down the gorgeous mountainside, back to the highway, which would certainly lead to a town, which would lead us yet to another town, and eventually, a city. Sometime in the near future, it would lead us to Bountiful and the Glad Tidings Assisted Living Home, where my new life awaited me.

That phrase again: my new life.

How strange it sounded! I am too old to start again. Yes. No. I do not know.

I had grown so comfortable in my old life.

And now, having driven across the plains, fished high in the mountains, bagged a peak, and spent a night shivering in a car stuck in a place that only the moon and stars could see, I am back on a paved road and headed in a direction that I have never quite been before.

This was the practical thing to do, I argue with myself. The time would come when I would need help in my daily tasks and routines. I would be closer to my family and be around people my own age. Yes, practical. And forward-thinking. Reasonable. Conventional. Sensible. What was expected of a man my age.

I think of my beloved plains.

There was nothing sensible about living on the plains. It is a hard country, too cold in the winter, too hot in the summer, too rocky, too flat, too small, and too large.

Yet I loved it there. I loved feeling as though I were on the edge of nature. I loved the people who had the heart and grit to live in such a fierce land. I loved being a part of my community and, with my medicines, making a difference to them. I loved the Church members there, some of them meeting in front rooms of small homes temporarily turned into chapels. I loved them because they came to church when it was thirty below and one hundred above and never thought it extraordinary. I loved them because they were like the plains themselves: unchangeable, unassuming, productive, and solid. It was difficult to leave them.

But the rational being brought me back and led me to this road, bound for Utah. In life, your loves come and go, and if you are fortunate, they last a long time, but in the end, they are all taken away from you or you from them, and you have just the promise of eternities and the faith that it will happen to help you stay whole. So you are left with photographs and memories, whispers, aches, and reminders of other days and other times.

So many of my loves were slipping away from me. It was like one door after another slowly closing until there were only doors open inches wide, and then, the final, soft click of the latch catching fast.

This is what it is to grow old. Maybe it suffices as a definition of growing old: more is taken from your life than comes into it. You feel as though you are being guided or pushed toward the outside rim of some unseen circle until, finally, you are at the edge and can only observe what takes place at the center, the center where you once were young, hopeful, vital, and energetic.

Where Levi is now, I thought.

I saw in him all the recklessness of a young man: from an electric, humorous, and occasionally self-absorbed being to one who was intuitive enough to put his arm around my shoulder, grasp my wrist, softly say, "Here," and show me how to cast a fly. And another side of his character, someone who thought, "Loyal is a man of the plains. I will take him to a mountain, we will climb it, and he will see something from the top of a peak that he only could have imagined before."

He and I are both now speeding toward our respective destinations. Levi back to school to finish his education and then bolting ahead with life and the possibility of a future with Miss Rachel, and me to the Glad Tidings Assisted Living Home. We both stand at the edge of something new.

And I sense this: both of us fear our destination. Yet neither of us have the will nor strength to alter our course. We are done in the plains. We are done in the streams. We are done in the mountains. We have only a road left to share. Ahead of us lies blue-black pavement, and with each mile we proceed toward our destinies, the opposite of what should happen in a perfect world is taking place.

We are, I believe, both becoming less certain of this road we are on. Whether it is faith or foolishness that keeps us on our south-southwest course, our backs to the sun, I cannot yet say.

CHAPTER TWENTY-FOUR
I Pitch a Fit and
Hurl My Car Keys into the Sagebrush

We got out of the mountains okay. Didn't see a bear. Cold, sure, but we had enough to eat and a lake to drink from, if it came to that. Three firefighters on patrol came up and pulled us out, and I was glad to see them, although they obviously thought I was some kind of fool from the city who didn't have the smarts to get out of the mountains when a storm was blowing my way.

Looking back, I guess they were right. I was distracted, which is an easy thing to be in mountains like those. I didn't have the sense to book it somewhere safe when the clouds rolled toward us. *A little common sense, Levi, can go a long way.*

Okay. Whew. It all becomes just another story. It had been an amazing few days since we left North Dakota. It seemed like that was a month ago, but it was only . . . only . . . I had lost track of time. What day was it? I really didn't know. Friday, Saturday? Somewhere toward the weekend. Where were we? In Wyoming now. I was pretty sure of that. *Bear down, Levi. Focus. Think it through. Breathe. In and out. Make the funny little triangle, like the way you're supposed to when your wife is in heavy labor and screaming nasty things at you.*

I take inventory.

We survived a tornado. Or an almost tornado.

We fell in love with a desk clerk with madness in her hair. Check that. I fell in love with a woman whose stack of hair would require a building code approval in most counties.

We fell out of love. Check that. I fell out of love with a desk clerk.

We got out of a biker bar alive.

We fished.

We climbed a mountain. Loyal's first.

We bought a pile of jerky, chips, and juice.

We talked about love. Twice. We talked about life. We talked about taking pictures of people.

We talked about happiness and success and the meaning of life. Light stuff like that.

We'd put well more than a thousand miles on the red car.

We got stuck.

We got unstuck.

And now there was only one thing left to do. It was as big as the mountains on either side of us as we headed down a long, curly road toward a high-desert valley below. Get Loyal to Utah. Then get myself back into school for my senior year. This whole adventure had come down to just that. *Get to where we each needed to be.*

I need to call Aunt Barbara. I do. She says she was worried but kept telling herself we probably were just living large, two guys on the road, making the most of the trip home.

So that's why she hasn't bothered calling.

Funny how someone like her could come from the genetic pool of Loyal and Daisy Wing.

I tell her okay, I understand, and now that we'd gone fishing and hiking and we are running out of miles between wherever we were and wherever we needed to get to, we'd probably just kind of head toward Utah, and she'd see her dad in a few days.

She asks me how much I had put on the card. I do some quick mental calculations and say, "About a thousand. Maybe closer to fifteen hundred."

She laughs. Nervously. She hopes I'll say, "Just kidding," but I don't. In the end, she just says, "Oh. Oh. Oh, okay. Okay. Yes, yes, okay."

Uncle Loyal and I just drove. We had maps in the glove compartment, but I didn't bother to look at them anymore. We just drove. We didn't talk as much as we had before. I just followed the white lines on the blue highways, and if there were a river or a mountain range or a pretty valley or a small town, I pointed the car toward it and we drove that way. We didn't need any more reason than that to get off the highway, take a back road, and see what everyone else seemed to be missing.

We just drove. We drove straight, we drove curly. We drove that red car into the ground.

We stopped to help people. We stopped *every time*, whenever a car was on the side of the road and people looked at us with hope and sadness and worry. We took off flat tires and put on spares. We walked to a creek with empty juice bottles and came back with cold water and poured it into a radiator. We made a call on a cell phone for a tow truck when we couldn't fix a bad water pump. We once took a man about my age and his young, pretty, new wife to the next town, where they talked with a mechanic and bartered a way to get their car fixed. I took a twenty-dollar bill out of my wallet and stuck it in his pocket when he wasn't looking, and he never knew what I had done. Once, Uncle Loyal just stood in front of a car, hood opened, staring at the engine. Then he asked for duct tape, and to my surprise the driver had some in a road emergency kit. Deftly, Uncle Loyal rolled the tape around a leaking hose and told the awed driver and his wife and their three kids to head to the nearest town and get the hose replaced but that the duct tape should hold until then.

We never mentioned our names; we never took any money. We just helped. We were all on this road. On it together, and although no two of us were headed to exactly the same spot, we all were headed home. *All of us.* I realized that sometimes we all break down along the road, and about all we can do is look to those zipping by with a bit of hope, an aching heart, and a prayer on our lips. Stopping and helping always made me feel good, and it distracted me from the ultimate purpose of this whole goofy trip. And the next vehicle to break down might have been ours. Would anyone stop? Would anyone help? Who knows? We *could* stop, so we did.

So we drove. Aimlessly but with a purpose. I had so much time to think. I felt like a knight on a white horse with nothing more to do than set the world straight. I was on a quest. I felt like Quixote. We drove. We drove. Then we drove some more. That's all I can really say about those few days, somewhere beyond the middle but not too close to the end. *We drove.*

Somewhere we realized it was Sunday, and we found a little church and stopped in, just in time for sacrament meeting. Uncle Loyal found a tie for me in his suitcase, and I scrounged up the closest thing I had to a dress shirt, put on the only long pants I had packed for what was to have been a two-day trip, tops, and we slipped into the back of the small chapel and then cut out of there almost as soon as the amen was said. And then we drove some more.

We drove through Yellowstone, I remember that. Uncle Loyal mentioned that he'd never been there, so I tuned in long enough to follow the signs through Cooke City, past the tall, silent mountains. Then we headed north again, clear back into Montana. We drove through a nice canyon with a beautiful little stream and ended up in a pretty town that was surrounded by mountains.

I got back on the freeway again, and we drove through the old mining town of Butte, and then I saw a sign on a highway that said "Idaho," and followed it to the south, then doubled back, then turned south again. We stayed at more shoddy motels, ate at little restaurants and cafés, and occasionally I parked somewhere on the side of the road, usually by a stream or in view of a mountain range, and we just stared and talked a little. I could feel things changing. I could feel myself changing. This road trip was doing something to me, and I wondered what and tried not to be scared, and hoped that it would all come down to something I could figure out and live with, something that was true for me.

I thought of Rachel. I thought of my parents. Something was here, large and real, but I didn't quite know what it was. I knew I was supposed to be learning something, that this trip was more than a coincidence, but the thoughts and the words and the feelings had not come all together for me. I knew I was close but not close enough. I knew I had to drive until it made sense and I understood what I was supposed to learn from this trip. *So we drove some more.*

We did this for two, three, maybe four days. It was all a blur.

And with each passing mile, something weighed on me.

I could no longer ignore it. It was clear. It was as unmistakable as the big gray mountains shimmering to my right and to my left as we drove through yet another high-plains valley.

I didn't want to take Uncle Loyal to Utah.

I didn't want to see him pigeonholed in the Glad Tidings Assisted Living Home.

I didn't like the idea of him playing shuffleboard with old men who couldn't remember his name and maybe not even their own. I didn't want him to be sitting in the lounge, waiting for Mia Maid classes to come and sing to him. I didn't want him to eat institutional food and use a walker to get around. I didn't want him to be goaded into bingo games by an activity director or lined up outside the building waiting for a bus to take him and the other residents shopping. I didn't even want him to be called a resident. I didn't want him to wake up at night and feel the awful pangs of being away from his brown house in North Dakota, away from his neighbors and the people who had depended on him for all of his adult life. I didn't want him to be so far from Glenn's grave. I didn't want him slumped in his chair, his mind turning to oatmeal as a television set flickered images and the laugh track on the program cackled. I didn't want any of that for him. He'd cared for people all his life, and now, when he needed it most, no one was caring for him.

And yet, here I was, delivering him to this fate. A pawn. I felt that I was a small cog in a very large machine, and even if, with all my will, I tried to throw a wrench into it, the gears would keep grinding and maybe chew up the wrench and me in the process. I felt helpless. I wanted to shout that something didn't feel right, but I didn't have the courage, and I wondered what others would think.

Did anyone understand? Couldn't someone help? *I'm broken down on the road. Please?* I was begging for something, and I couldn't quite figure out what. Why was no one stopping to help? I was on the side of the road, my engine all but shut down, waiting in vain for someone to stop. *Why?* Didn't Uncle Loyal and I stop for everyone?

I felt awful about it. I felt as though my hands were dirty. I wanted to drive into Utah, stop someplace that was really busy, point to Uncle Loyal, and shout, "This is Loyal! He is a man of the plains! He knows more than just about anyone I've ever met! He is wise beyond your understanding! You will not put him in a box and let him waste away! He has too much to give! *He is a human being!*"

Of course, if I did that, I would be the one who was institutionalized.

And who was I really shouting at anyway?

No one, that's who. And maybe everyone.

What to do? What to do?

Drive. That was the only answer I could come up with. Just drive, fill up the car with gas, and drive some more. And hope that some answer would come of all this, an answer as big and unmistakable as the thunderstorm that trapped us in the mountains or caught us on the plains.

So I drove. The more I drove, the less we spoke. Uncle Loyal could tell that I wasn't myself, that I was feeling heavy and troubled. And I am sure that he knew the cause of my misery. More than once, he leaned my way and simply said, "It will be okay, Levi. It will work out," and then he'd pat me on the knee.

I couldn't drive around forever, conveniently ignoring the circumstances. In the deeper part of my consciousness, I knew I *had* to get back to school, *had* to graduate, and I *had* to see Rachel and find out what was in store for us. If I could only find a way to blend what I *had* to do with what I wanted for Uncle Loyal, then maybe I wouldn't have felt as though this predicament and my role in it weren't slowly strangling me.

I found myself driving through a long valley in southern Idaho. At its pointy end, the mountains loomed, and I could see the road climbing up into them. The signs started to include the mileage to Tremonton, Ogden, and Salt Lake City. It was as if a kind of unrelenting gravitational pull was tugging us toward home.

We pass a small reservoir on our left, then a small town on our right. Outside, high, gray clouds obscure the sun. The wind is blowing hard; I can see trees tilting and feel the occasional jolt when a strong gust slammed into our car. Uncle Loyal stares out the window and says little.

I see the sign ahead that welcomes us to Utah. I slow the car and drift toward the side of the road until we gradually come to a stop. I turn off the ignition and keep my eyes straight ahead.

Uncle Loyal looks at me and says pleasantly, "Levi, shall I plan to walk the rest of the way to Bountiful?"

"I'm not going to do it."

"Do what, Levi?"

"I'm not going to be the one who drives you to the Glad Tidings or Good Tidings or Bad Tidings or whatever it is. I'm not going to be the one who puts you in a box with three squares a day and watches as you rot. I'm not going to. I can't. No one can make me. *It's wrong.*"

"Well," Uncle Loyal says, and from the corner of my eye I can see he is nodding. "Well. It appears we have a problem or two to work out. Levi, we have issues."

I have to smile at that. "Yeah. We have issues."

"So what shall we do? It seems that we have few options."

"This is what we do."

I open the door and walk around to the front of the car. A big semitruck blows by, and little pieces of gravel spray over me, stinging my face and my right arm. I take the keys to the car and face the open country, and I fling them high and far out into the sagebrush. I hear them tinkle and see them bounce as they hit the ground. I glare out into the sage. It felt good. Pointless, I know. Too much drama, yeah. But it made me feel better. I had taken a stand. I couldn't quite say what I had taken a stand against, but I had.

A gust of wind blows from across the sagebrush plain and knocks me off balance. I stagger back to the driver's side of the car, open the door, and climb in.

"There. We have no more issues. We're stuck here. We can go no farther. Can't drive into Utah without the car keys. Problem solved."

I steal a glance at Uncle Loyal. To my relief, he doesn't look upset or annoyed or angry. He just looks like Uncle Loyal. The sparkle in his eyes. The edges of his mouth curled into a bemused slip of a smile.

"We have to go somewhere . . . eventually," he suggests in a sweet way. "We cannot stay here interminably, eh? We will need food, water, and shelter. Our jerky supply, I'm afraid, is running low."

"Jerky. Yeah. We need more jerky. I suppose. I guess. But for now, this is good. I'm not hungry. Are you hungry? You can have my share of the jerky. This is really good, just sitting here. I'll have time to think. I've got to think our way out of this, Uncle Loyal."

So I sit there, eyes closed, and think. Nothing comes to me. Every time I start on a possible solution, something prevents me from going any further with it. Take him back to North Dakota? He'd be happy there, but he had no place to live, and Aunt Barbara wouldn't be pleased about me not delivering her pops. And kiss good-bye the six hundred bucks. Find him another place to live? No. What's the point of that? Glad Tidings might be the best spot for him. I didn't have a firsthand tabulation of the pros and cons of nursing homes in the Salt Lake Valley. Have him move in with Barbara and Warren? No, they'd probably already thought of that and decided it wouldn't work. Every exit ramp off the road led to a dead end.

Uncle Loyal finally asks me a one-word question. "Thoughts?"

"Nothing seems like it's going to work. This all just feels *wrong*."

"I'll be fine, Levi. You'll be fine. This is life, and we must move on. We can't bow out and just stop, tempting though it may be at times."

"I know. I know. But this isn't right."

"It is likely my only option, or at least the best option I have. My gratitude for your concern knows no bounds. It has been . . ." and he stops, and he looks out across the dry sagebrush steppe, "It has been so long since anyone has shown so much interest in and care for me."

"And for me, it's been so long since anyone has taught me so much, especially in such a short time. We're a good team, Uncle Loyal."

"Yes. A good team. A very good team. So what do we do?"

I fold my arms and scowl. I understand that this roughly represented the attitude and actions of a five-year-old throwing a temper tantrum, but it didn't matter. I had earned this chance to power whine. You've got to take a stand, right? Sometimes you have to say, "This isn't right, and I'm not going along with it." I keep coming back to the word *right*. It seems so clear, the right and the wrong here. I *have* to act on it. Isn't that what we're taught since we're Sunbeams? I was at that point. Maybe I was just a small cog in a big machine, but when even a small cog doesn't do its job, it can cause the whole thing to grind to a halt.

Small cogs count too. Maybe I wouldn't be ground into powder.

"I guess we just sit until we think of something better," I say, letting out a hissing sound as I speak. I wrap my fingers around the steering wheel in a death grip.

"That might be a while."

"Yes. It might be. We spent one night in the car, and in a worse place than this. We can do it again. Room on wheels. Levi and Loyal rule. The road kings."

"Doubtlessly, we'd eventually attract the attention of local law enforcement officials. They tend to notice cars stopped on the side of the road."

"I guess so. Yeah, you're right."

"Then what? This is a fine predicament we find ourselves in."

"We make a run for it. They ain't takin' us alive, Ma! We make a beeline across the sagebrush, head for the border. We crawl low, so they can't see us there. We paint our faces with mud so that we blend in. We become desert ghosts. We hole up somewhere. We get ourselves nicknames, like Butch and Poncho. We get inside their heads. We grow beards, let our hair go, and rob the Wells Fargo stagecoach."

"I like the sound of it. I had never considered a career as an outlaw. Although we eventually would be apprehended. Or worse. And I haven't seen a single stagecoach on our entire journey. They may be obsolete, Levi. We may be buying into a dead industry. Just a thought."

"But what a life we'd have until then."

"And Rachel? Do you think you could coax her into becoming an outlaw's wife? And your choice of careers might considerably alter your chance at a temple marriage and sealing."

"She could start her own band of outlaws. The Wild Women. The Daughters of Ishmael. Or something like that. She'll be Bad Rachel. We could be on the cover of magazines. We'd be famous. They'd make action hero figures based on us. You could be played by Robert DeNiro."

"Very well. Who is this Robert De Nardo?"

"Never mind. And I'd share all the booty with the poor and the needy. Orphans. Widows. High priests who can't remember their names."

"Very noble of you."

"Noble. Yep. That'll be us. The L&L Gang. Noblest of the bad guys. We could run for Congress, too."

Uncle Loyal pauses a few seconds and then looks at me. He folds his spotty brown hands on his lap and sighs.

"It won't work, Levi. I am sorry to be the bearer of bad news. But your plan will not succeed. Neither of us fits the criminal profile. And a life of crime, I assume, is hard, a difficult way of existing, indeed." He looks at me with a slight smile. "We have but one choice. Shall we go look for the keys?"

I let go of the steering wheel. Of course, he was right. Of course, it was only make-believe; I was trying to inject a little humor in a bleak situation. It was silly. But it's how I deal with stuff. I knew the answer, at least the short-term answer.

"Okay. We don't have a choice. Let's go look for the keys."

So we climb out of the car and into the blustery wind. I have to admit that when I chucked the keys into the sagebrush, I sort of kept track of where they landed, just in case. Finding the keys wouldn't be hard, and it takes only a couple of minutes before I see them glinting in the late-afternoon haze and reach down for them by a little clump of wheatgrass.

Uncle Loyal's always-calming effect had worked its magic again, but I was firm in my conviction about two things. One, I wished for something else, a way to keep him happy, close, alive, and vital, keep that river of wisdom flowing, at some other place than the care home; and two, I was not going to be the one who drove him across the state line into Utah.

Call it a point of pride or honor or stubbornness, but it represented something to me, although just what symbolism it carried I couldn't quite figure out. Maybe it was as simple as not wanting to be the one who delivered him to what likely would be his end, but I felt it was something much deeper.

We get back to the car. Uncle Loyal starts toward the passenger side, just where he'd been for eighteen hundred miles. The red car is a mess—mud from the mountains, bugs splattered across the grille and windshield, the inside filled with empty bags of chips and jerky, pop and juice cans scattered in the backseat.

I walked a few steps behind him toward the passenger door. Uncle Loyal looks at me with an unspoken question.

"Here you go, Poncho." To his surprise, I flip the keys to him, and he reaches out with his left hand and catches them. At least I had settled on one thing.

"Your turn, Uncle Loyal. You get to drive the chuck wagon home."

CHAPTER TWENTY-FIVE

MILE BY MILE, WE COME CLOSER TO BOUNTIFUL

THERE IS LITTLE THAT SURPRISES me in life. I am, I believe, an observer of human beings. I see patterns in our behavior. I understand, I believe, most things about most people. It comes from years of watching and years of thinking about what I've seen.

But I confess to being taken aback when Levi tossed me the car keys and instructed me to get us home, and I also wondered about the word *home*, which in another hour or so would take on an entirely different meaning for me.

I thought of my old Dakota house, windswept, on the prairie. Maybe the fleeting thought of wind on my face caused me to do what I did next.

I meekly climb behind the steering wheel, adjust the mirrors, and start the car's engine. The accelerator roars at the light touch of my foot. It is a very fast, powerful, and filthy car. I cautiously pull into the traffic, and then, perhaps in retribution for Levi's surprise to me, I jam my foot on the gas pedal, while he, at first, ignores me, then grins slightly, then becomes wild-eyed with joy. As we used to say in my youth, I laid rubber with a screech that brought me something akin to joy.

He looks my way. "Well?"

"One hundred and five, Levi. I am sorry."

"And you were worried about a life of crime. You said we weren't cut out for it."

"I just wanted to see how fast this car would go. Now I know. At least one hundred and five. I will now begin the repentance process by confessing my sin: I am speeding. Remorse comes next, but it may take a while. This is rather fun. Quite enjoyable, in fact."

"You are definitely speeding."

I ease up on the accelerator, but Levi's smile stays in place for twenty miles.

The tall mountains loom to my left. I feel comforted by them after my experiences in Montana and Wyoming. We pass several towns. We pass an old mill with many colorful slogans spray-painted on it, many of them seeming to welcome missionaries home. A strange custom, I think. We pass tall power lines appearing as gaunt giants with arms spread wide to hold electrical lines. We pass the Great Salt Lake, its murky waters lapping the shore. We pass subdivisions tucked next to the freeway and a ceaseless string of billboards. We pass a huge lot filled with junked cars. We pass many car dealerships. We pass gleaming little chapels, their spires tall and white in the fading evening light. The cars around me drive bullet-fast, and I conclude that use of turn signals must be optional according to Utah law. And the song of the wheels on the road, spinning over and over, seems to repeat in oily cadence, "a mile, a mile, a mile, a mile . . ."

The signs tell us that Salt Lake City is growing close. At a town called Layton, Levi asks if I will pull over. I do, and he suggests that we trade places. I do not fully understand why, unless it's a matter of practicality; he knows the way to Barbara's home, and I do not. But his movement and his voice suggests something more. My guess: we have traveled almost two thousand miles together in the red car, and perhaps he feels that he should finish the mission, distasteful though it might be for him. I remember similar feelings when my Daisy passed on. To finish, to finish. We must always finish.

So he takes control of the car and gets off on one of the exits that says Bountiful. We wind our way up a steep drive. To the south, I see a golf course stretching along the hillside. Levi tells me that Barbara's house is not very far from where we are. Our long journey had been condensed to mere minutes.

I look back over my shoulder as we drive higher on the hill on our way to Bountiful. The lake stretches out for miles. Long-fingered rays of the sun skip over the water. The air is hazy. The first lights of the evening glow in the gathering brown dusk.

I try to think of this as my new place, my new home, somewhere I can and will be happy. I close my eyes and concentrate.

But all I can see in my mind are fields of corn swaying in a midsummer's morning, sticky hot, under an eggy-blue sky, and I cannot help but think, *I wonder if a storm will rise tonight.* The skin on my arms and face feels gritty, and even the cool air from the car's vents does little to make me feel comfortable.

If I could only hear a meadowlark sing, I think, *I would feel much better, feel much more at home.*

CHAPTER TWENTY-SIX

THIS MAN CALLED LOYAL, WHO HE IS

THIS MAN LOYAL. I DIDN'T even know him a week ago. Who is he? I think I know.

He is kind and wise, and he never wanted anything beyond what he needed.

He is true to the woman he married, even though she is gone.

He never hurt a soul.

He helps the ill.

He binds the wounds of others.

He comforts those who mourn.

He speaks softly.

He acts gently.

He never had a bad thought about anyone.

He never had a bad word about anyone.

He sees the best in everyone.

He knows the stars in the heavens, the birds in the skies, the plants beneath his feet.

He knows contentment.

He knows the secrets of life but will let you discover them on your own.

He knows peace.

He climbs mountains.

He is a fisherman.

He is a man of the plains.

He laughs.

He hasn't watched television in five years.

He doesn't know what an iPad is.

He doesn't care to know what an iPad is.

He drives too fast.

He moves slowly but with a purpose and with grace.

He taught me the amazing power of slowness.

He is unbelievably, amazingly, and extraordinarily cool, and he doesn't even know it.

He knows what matters.

He knows what counts.

We're friends.

And now, here I am, pulling around the corner, spying Aunt Barbara and Uncle Warren's house. I'll drop him off. I'll say good-bye. I'll drive to my home. And quite possibly never get rid of the gnawing feeling in my stomach that I'm doing something that, while maybe not wrong, is far from being right.

Chapter Twenty-Seven
A Note on the Door
and Things Change, but Only a Little

I recall Barbara and Warren's house. Somewhat, at least. I know it is large and white and has two columns on the porch and that it faces west, toward the lake. It is high on the hill. Barbara and Warren seem successful, and I am glad for them.

The red car doesn't seem to move so fast now. It is a steep hill, and I fear Levi and I have been rough on the car. Yet I have a stray thought, one that makes no sense and yet also makes much sense: the flashy red car is probably a better vehicle now than when Levi steered it down my street in North Dakota. It's broken in. It's added a few miles. It has a few healthy rattles.

I see the house. It looks different. A new coat of paint, a light tan. The lawn is sculpted. The grounds immaculate. I try to remember what Barbara and Warren do for a living. Something with travel, I think, but I really can't recall. I must remember to not add my Dakotan "eh?" to the end of sentences. Although she has never said it, I can tell it ruffles Barbara.

Levi guides the car to the curb. This is where it all begins for me. I will go in and see Barbara and her family. We'll have supper, most likely; inevitably, though, the time will come, the minute will arrive, in which she says to me, "Dad, let's go take a look at Glad Tidings. I think you'll be surprised. Let's run you over there and get you acquainted with the place."

And I will nod, docile in my manner, and say, "Yes. That would be fine. I'd like to see it." Then we will go.

Levi clears his throat. He looks at me, then he looks toward the door of Barbara's house.

"I'll go too," he says. "I'll go with you up to the house."

"Thank you."

We slowly climb out of the car and trudge up the walkway, up the stairs toward the front door. I see an envelope taped to the door. Levi walks a little ahead of me and reaches for it. I see the envelope has his name written on it in bold, black letters.

He reads the note, then comes back to me.

"Hmmmpf. Some emergency at work, I guess. Aunt Barbara apologizes. She says that she won't be here for quite a while. She's got to get some people out of Mexico. Hurricane is coming in, and they're all panicking. She and Warren are stuck until late. She wants me to take you to Glad Tidings. She said she called Glad Tidings on her way to work and they're expecting you. Hmmmpf. Imagine that. Looks like we get to take one more drive together, Uncle Loyal."

I cannot even begin to tell him how happy that makes me.

CHAPTER TWENTY-EIGHT

MY BEST IDEA EVER IN THE WORLD

I WAS NOT EXACTLY HAPPY about having to take Uncle Loyal to the Glad Tidings Retirement Nursing Home Assisted Living Put-'em-in-a-Box Golden and Twilight Years Home for Old People. Put it this way: I summoned the last of my courage and nerve to get him to Aunt Barbara's, not to mention sticking my heart on ice cubes. My part was over. My job was done. *Remember, Levi, this was a business transaction, and good businessmen don't get wrapped up in emotions.* They don't think too hard about people and their situations. They don't pay attention to feelings. They don't get *involved.* If they did, they wouldn't be in business for long. Look at my dad. Yes, look at him . . . the photographer. I guess he's stayed in business, but he barely makes a living. Scrapes by. You don't want to be like him, right? *So don't get so emotional about this, Levi. Conform. Forget about those things you talked over with Loyal.*

My hands might have been dirty, but I was only doing what was expected of me. What I agreed to do. *What I was getting paid for.*

Paid for. What I didn't say to Loyal, and what I hope he didn't see, was that the check for six hundred bucks, made out to yours truly, was tucked inside the note about the emergency in Mexico. I've never told Uncle Loyal I was getting paid for this trip, although he probably knew I was on the Barbara-and-Warren payroll. Anyway, I slid the envelope into my pants pocket, where it felt as though it weighed twenty pounds.

Barbara had also left directions in the envelope on how to get to Glad Tidings. It wasn't far away.

"The journey's not over, eh?" Uncle Loyal asks, and there was a hopeful sound to his question.

"No. Not yet. Not quite. I guess I take you to Glad Tidings."

He looks pleased. "The trip isn't done. Good. Very good. This road trip has been quite the experience for me. I have enjoyed it immensely. I'll gladly go a few miles more with you."

I start down the hill toward the town and the great lake. I can't say I'm in a good mood. My thoughts are dark, and I'm not feeling too terrific about myself. I had been lured into making this trip by the promise of a quick cash infusion to support my dwindling finances.

I had done this for fast money.

And then things got complicated.

I ended up liking Loyal. I ended up liking him a lot. *I ended up loving him.* And that's where everything got goofy. If I'd been able to keep this a simple cash transaction, service provided, service paid for, Business 101 class, if I'd been able to keep my emotions out of it, if Uncle Loyal had been a doddering old fool, then all of this would have been different.

But did I want it to be different? Would I have exchanged my experiences driving across the plains with Uncle Loyal, and then driving over the mountains, fishing, getting stuck, pitching my keys into the brush, seeing Yellowstone, and the other thousand small experiences for anything?

No. Not at all. So in one sense, maybe it all worked out as it was meant to.

But now we are at the end. He is going to spend the remainder of his days at Glad Tidings; I am going to head back to school, graduate next spring, and then start my career, whatever that meant. The end. The end of our road trip. And while I may not be a hundred-watt bulb, I am bright enough to know how easily we slip from one world to another, and how the bridges between people, while they're hardly ever burned, do just rust away with time.

I am only half paying attention to Aunt Barbara's instructions, but I knew we're getting close. We cross South Davis, then Orchard Boulevard, continuing our downward direction. We'll be there in five minutes if the instructions are right.

And then something hits me. It hits me with the force of an eight-on-the-Richter-scale earthquake. It seemed like a bright ball of light, pushed by a stiff wind, rolling right toward me from the mountains far to the west, across the lake, blasting up and slapping me across the face. Suddenly, the day is bright again. I feel an incredible surge of joy, a sense of rightness, a solution to the problem. I went from feeling as though I were the gallows master to feeling like an angel of light.

I pull the car off the side of the road, into a big-box store parking lot. My hands are trembling as I put the car in park. Uncle Loyal looks at me with a deep, gentle gaze, his eyebrows raised slightly in an unasked question.

"I've got it! I know what we should do! Why didn't I think of this before?!"

"And what is your idea, if I may ask?"

"This is so cool."

"Yes, I'm sure it is."

"This is the best idea ever. I mean *ever*. In twenty-four years of thinking, this is it. My best idea ever. Did I say that? My crowning achievement. It is the *answer*."

"The answer to what, Levi?"

"The answer to the problem. Your problem. My problem. *This is what we need to do.*"

"I am eager to hear what you have arrived at."

"This is it. You move into *my* apartment this fall. We have a place with four bedrooms, and the last time I checked, only three were taken. You become," and I pause for dramatic effect, "*my roommate!*"

He didn't say anything. It was a funny moment, all right, in the big store's parking lot, the engine running, traffic passing by, life passing by, and a solution to this ugly problem at hand. I hoped that Uncle Loyal would be as pumped about it as I was.

He isn't.

"I'm not certain that would work," he murmurs.

"Work? Of course it would work! This is so elegant. It answers *everything!* You become one of the guys, the buds, a dude. You stay at home and maybe keep the place looking good, and we come back at night and just hang. Like what we've been doing this last week. Only in a place with no wheels. It just goes on and on. It doesn't change. A road trip without the road. You'd have a place to live. We could fish anytime we wanted. We could watch baseball on TV. Cable. We have cable, Uncle Loyal! There's a nice trout stream ten minutes from town. And the girls—they'd really dig it with you there. You'd be everyone's grandfather."

I try to think of the right words to convey to him how perfect this would be. *Loyal as my roommate.* I search for the right phrase, the right words, the right intonation to sway him. "You'd be a chick magnet!"

Well, maybe it wasn't a case of clear, convincing logic, but it was true. The girls would love Uncle Loyal. And if they loved him, maybe they'd love me if things didn't work out with Rachel. Share the love, Uncle Loyal. *Feel the love.* We'd be unbeatable.

"I assume that means I would help you and your roommates secure dates with young ladies, eh?" he says.

"Yep. Bottom line. In a nutshell. That about sums it up."

The words are gushing out of my mouth. The more I talk about it, the more I felt it was the right thing to do. Think of how cool it would be to take Loyal to church with me on Sundays. Of course, he would need to go to a real ward most of the time, and not a student ward, but he could drop in occasionally. He'd be right there for me, my roommates, for all of us. And it would be a lot cheaper for him to live with us than at the Glad Tidings Assisted Living Home. All the angles were covered. It all felt so good, and since I was a three-year-old in Primary, I'd been taught about feeling good and doing the right thing. This nailed them both.

"Do you see it, Uncle Loyal? This *would work.* I think Barbara would even go for it too. You'd still be close to her."

My words hang still in the air. Only a few seconds go by, but it seems like an hour. I can see Uncle Loyal thinking about what I had said. I could tell he was considering it. I understood that the whole notion is interesting to him. *He was seriously trying to figure out if it would work.*

"It feels right," I say slowly, quietly, trying to close the deal.

Finally he turns toward me. There we are in the dirty red car, hardly recognizable from the flashy, souped-up vehicle I had rolled down his old street in North Dakota. So much had changed. I am a different person than the one who picked him up a week ago.

Uncle Loyal's eyes are sad, and his chin seems to quiver. "I'm sorry, Levi. I can't. I just can't. It would upset so many things. But you'll never know how much you honor me to even suggest this thing. How I have loved these days on the road with you. How I have learned to respect and love you."

No, no, no! This was it. This was our *answer.* I tell Uncle Loyal just that.

Again, silence, as all that wisdom rattles around in his head and he carefully selects his words.

"It just won't work out, Levi. I am sorry. So terribly sorry. The age difference . . ." and he stops for a few seconds. "Well, it just would not be the way you envision. It is so complicated. Barbara and Warren have selected a place for me. Now, I must go to it."

"Can you think about it? If you don't like this Glad Tidings joint, call me, let me know. I can come up in a heartbeat and break you out of there. You know I will. You know it."

"Yes, I do. I know that. What a measure of a friendship, to unconditionally help another. I know that there are few things you wouldn't do for me. And I for you."

The traffic is heavier. I want to stay right there, in the big-box store parking lot, where we are at least out of the flow. I have no desire to get back into the thick rush of things, the race, the competition, the rocky road ahead on my way to become . . . to become something and someone to make my mark in the world, even if it were a tiny smudge. But what did Uncle Loyal teach me, what did he say? You gain more by wanting less. That we all could be photographers. That peace and contentment are gifts. That tiny things really are big things.

If I am a smudge, I'm going to be a happy smudge and do my part well.

It was Loyal who finally said it.

"I think it's time that we press on. It would be wonderful to get to Glad Tidings before daylight leaves us."

I can see my choices are limited. We could spend the night stuck in the mountains, we could spend the night off to the side of the road, but we can't spend the night in a parking lot in Bountiful, minutes from the Glad Tidings terrace.

"If we have to."

"I think we do. We must. But I want you to remember this. I was tempted. Sorely tempted to take you up on your kind offer," Uncle Loyal says softly. "I believe I would have relished, as you said it, being a chick magnet, a role that I have never been cast in. And at my age. A delightful thought, Levi. Simply wondrous."

I put the road-weary red car into gear and, less than three minutes later, spot the long, curving driveway of the Glad Tidings Assisted Living facility. The grounds are filled with blooming rose bushes, grass that is still mostly green, and a few tall trees. It looks well kept and, considering what it is, somewhat inviting.

"We're home," I say glumly.

It's a three-story building, painted white, with long rows of square windows. Some of the rooms at the top have little balconies outside a sliding glass door. The building itself faces to the south—I guess good for sunshine in the winter, but it was clear Uncle Loyal would not have much of a view of the mountains or of the lake.

"Yes, home," he says softly. "We might as well go in."

We pull up under the overhang at the front of the building. We climb out of the car and pass through the automatic sliding glass doors. To our right is a desk with a receptionist. She looks up at us and says, "Good evening. May I help you?" Her name tag reads, "Heather."

Uncle Loyal looks around the lobby, taking it all in. Then he focuses on Heather and says what I knew he would say.

"My name is Loyal. I believe arrangements have been made through my daughter, Barbara Bates, for me to take up residence here."

"Oh. Okay. Let me see. Your name again?"

"Loyal. I am Loyal."

"Excuse me. Loyal?"

"Yes, Loyal."

"Will you be staying with us tonight?"

Uncle Loyal looks around at the lobby again. Lots of plastic ferns and flowers, and big prints of children playing or walking near a pond. A huge aquarium with brightly colored, vacuous fish idly swimming. A natural-gas fireplace, and even on a warm August evening, the small flame flickers yellow and blue. The light is subdued. Elevator music hums aimlessly through speakers in the ceiling. I see a line of wheelchairs near the entrance to a large room, probably where the residents eat their meals. Heather, the woman helping us, is clean, polite, and I think, somewhat mean-hearted, and likely made mostly of synthetic material. Her smile was so big that her toes must have been curling. The aroma in the lobby is an off-the-shelf concoction, smelling only a little like oranges, more of antiseptic.

This is as far away from the plains of North Dakota as you could get.

I would have given anything for a blast of icy wind at that moment. Or even a jaw-dropping rattler of a thunderstorm. I would cheer the sight of a funnel cloud.

"Yes. I'll be staying," Uncle Loyal says, then, drawing in his breath, and with what I believe to this moment was a forced smile, he adds, "This is my new home."

"Let me make a call and have someone show you to your new room." She efficiently pushes a button on the desk console and says quietly, "William, we have a new resident at the front desk. Can you come and help him find his way?"

I guess I don't remember much about the next hour or so. Maybe I chose not to remember. I do know that my heart broke a little more each minute I was there. William came, tan, dressed in a blue uniform, grinned a glittering grin, and welcomed us. We went to the car and grabbed Uncle Loyal's belongings. A lifetime, I thought, and this is what it comes down to. Boxes and a pair of suitcases. Everything he needed, really. Loyal is a simple man.

William showed us Uncle Loyal's room, and about all I recall of it was that it was painted in neutral tones and seemed bland. Uncle Loyal exchanged pleasant chatter with William, who was just a little too slick for my tastes. Soon we are back on the elevator on our way down, and Loyal, true to form, is more worried about me than himself.

"I'll be fine here," Uncle Loyal says placidly. "Just fine. The people seem nice. I'll get along well, I believe. Perhaps I will make new friends."

"Yeah. Sure. You will. You're Loyal. How could *you* not?"

He looks directly at my face. He seems to be studying me as though trying to figure out what I'm thinking. And for the first time on the trip, he starts to say something, stops, starts again, and gets tangled in his words.

I think, *Sometimes you don't need to talk to have a conversation.*

The music gushes from the sound system. Violins. Syrupy and sweet.

"I cannot . . ." his voice sounds as dry as a plains wind blowing through a field of cornstalks. "Thank you, Levi, for the last week. You are that shooting star in my life. What an adventure. Our very own road trip. I will cherish the experience forever."

"So will I. It's been . . ." *What am I trying to say? Think, Levi. Keep it simple. Okay.* It comes down to this. Nothing more than this, and all of this, at the same time. "I've made a friend, Uncle Loyal. A good friend. That doesn't happen too often in this life. I know that already."

We stand in front of the fireplace, the soft heat rising. This is it. This is the good-bye. This is what I have been dreading, what I have been fighting for almost two thousand miles. *The very horrible moment of separation.*

"You need to push ahead, I suspect. Your parents have missed you and may be worried. Barbara will check in with me later. I will be well, Levi. And you need to find out if your world lights up when you see a certain young lady. Eh?"

"I know. Maybe Rachel is the one."

"No worries?"

"No," I lie. Honestly, I am worried about everything.

And I mean *everything.*

School, career, people, Rachel, family, and certainly, not least of all, Uncle Loyal. I needed something to tie it all down. Something to help me make sense of all of this.

I hold out my hand, and Uncle Loyal clasps it warmly. I am surprised, although I shouldn't have been, at the firmness of his grip. He is a man of the plains, after all, strong because of the wind and broiling sun and cutting blizzards. Strong because of his experience, what he knew, what he understood. Strong because of his wisdom, and strong because he was not only a man of the plains but a plain man.

His was a life of simple, plain, pure beauty. The way I now understood I wanted mine to turn out. I also want to be a beautifully plain man. Can you be a plain man and a shooting star at the same time? I think so. It doesn't sound possible, but I think it can be done. Maybe one comes because of the other. Maybe they are linked.

He lowers his head and says, "Good-bye, Levi. My best wishes to you, always. My brotherly love to you, always. All will be well, eh?"

"Good-bye, Loyal." I step away from him and walk a couple of steps.

"Levi," he calls. "Do you know what your name means in Hebrew? It means *joined*."

I look back at him and nod. *Joined*. I thought of all the miles we drove together. How fitting. How right, because through this incredible trip, we had become joined, as any two people must be who travel over long, hard roads together. It was the last piece of wisdom that Loyal imparted to me. Then I turn slowly and walk toward the glass doors. *Eh.*

I did not turn around to look back again. I could not.

I thought of all I had seen and experienced on this journey. I thought of the thunder, the lightning, of Evelyn, of Libby and her broken-down old boyfriend. I thought of Glenn and what a fine man he must have been. I thought of Daisy and how Loyal loved her. I thought of Jason and Marty and the three firefighters who pulled us out of the mud. I thought of the thuggy people in the bar and how they also had something to give. I thought of all the faces of all the people we stopped to help. And it hits me again: all of them crossed my path for a reason. I understood that it's not a short trip here and there, but a long and sometimes dangerous journey and we need to help each other, *belong* to each other, to arrive at our destinies. None of us can stand alone.

I thought of all those things and more, and then I arrive at the desk.

I reach into my pocket and pull out the envelope. Heather looks up at me, a question in her eyes. I had one of my own.

"Do you have a shredder?"

"Yes, we do."

"Would you mind running this through for me?"

"Not at all. I'll take care of it right now."

And the *zazzing* of the machine eating the envelope, check inside, sounds to me like freedom.

I thought of what was ahead of me. Studies and books and exams, places to go, acquaintances to make. Appointments to keep. Meetings and responsibilities. Men and women with fancy and impressive degrees and credentials, all climbing up, ever up, in a restless search for a false peace, using one another as objects, mere objects. Appearances and more appearances and then thinking even more about appearances. The shoulder-sagging worries about impressions and saying the right thing and being seen in the right places. The specter of ambition and pride and greed and having so much yet still wanting more was so real that I could feel it, see it, touch it if I wanted, as it beckoned me with a long, thin, bony hand.

"No thank you," I mumble, a little surprised at the sound of my own hoarse voice.

No thank you at all.

What have I learned? What have I learned? I have not made this long journey for no reason. May God never allow me to stop learning from the things I experience.

This world may be flat, but I don't have to be. I can stand tall, stand out, be someone and do something. I believe I am young enough to learn how to take and make photographs, but not necessarily the kind you shoot with a camera. I want my life to be filled with pretty pictures that are both plain and true. I want to be wise.

And a white-hot fierce feeling swells within me. It is clear and strong, heaven sent. I know what I am supposed to learn during this long journey. I have figured it out. *It is my truth.*

I will beg no man again. I will chart my course and never vary. I will take the back roads whenever I can, wherever they lead me. I will travel to the tops of peaks and along the valley floors. I will stop to help those who have broken down along the side of the road, and I will seek nothing in return. I will be true to myself in every way.

I will be Loyal.

About the Author

Donald Smurthwaite is a native of Portland, Oregon. He and his wife, Shannon, are the parents of four children, whom he always will consider his best works. He has written eight novels, a couple dozen short stories, and lots of magazine stories, some of which were actually pretty good. He writes splendidly about golf, although he has grown ambivalent about the game in his middle-aged years. He runs ten miles a week and makes killer chocolate chip cookies, and yes, there is a connection between the two. He answers every fan letter or e-mail he receives. Lately, that hasn't been much of a workload.